Hope

Beckons

By Beth Trennepohl

Cover Design: Beth Trennepohl

Proofing & Editing: Kelli Bullard & Trish "The Ticket" Lewis

Author's photo credit: Teresa Boness

To:

From:

Dedication

For Gayle and Shirley,
who activated and inspired this
book.

Prologue

The Author Beckons ...

Expectations

Expectations are funny. If we have them and they are met, we expect them to be met again and again. But if they aren't met, we have to deal with the emotional backlash of dashed hopes and disappointment. I must have had a lot of disappointment in my childhood because I learned very early on to manage my expectations in order to maintain a sense of peace and order. But then, like many of us do, I carried this childhood framework into adulthood, not aware it was no longer necessary.

What I had learned to do as a child continued to be an invisible rule in my adult mind. It was simple and it worked for almost everything. It went like this: "Ignore the things you can't control." It wasn't a choice I made; it was automatic.

If I felt helpless, I would ignore the situation.

If I didn't see a way to help, serve, solve, or resolve — ignore.

If I felt my participation might cause conflict or complication — ignore.

The irony of the situation is that a rule about ignoring things kept me from seeing the consequences. It took a long time for this rule to cause enough consequences to get noticed. I vaguely remember the day I realized this. It was faint, but I noticed.

I took my youngest son to his first day of kindergarten, and I didn't feel a single twinge of emotion. I looked around at all the other mothers; that was when I became conscious of it. Some were crying. Some were overjoyed. I felt nothing. And of course, I *almost* ignored it.

I didn't realize how much the rule had affected me emotionally.

Feelings of disappointment: ignore. Loneliness: ignore. Embarrassment: ignore.

Love: ignore!

Love is where I began to feel the rub.

It was like the beginning of a blister forming on my heart where my old rule didn't fit anymore. That week I attended a Bible study by a new author, Ann Billington. She'd just written *Freedom From Your Past* with co-author Jimmy Evans.

Ann was a counselor at the church I attended, and over the course of the next year we met several times. She taught me we cannot turn off the things we don't want to feel and turn on the things we do. "Feelings don't have hot and cold spigots," I remember her saying. "They are either on or off; we can't pick and choose."

Awareness

Awareness is funny, too. When we increase awareness, things always get worse before they get better. I started to become aware of lots of things, but with Ann's help, I quit ignoring and began to feel them — first the bad, and eventually the good, too. I could cry, and I thought it would never stop, but it did. And then I could dream. And then I could love!

I'd love to tell you she was like my fairy godmother who showed up and waved her wand and made me ball-ready in a flash. But it didn't work that way for me. It was a slow process with lots of awareness and lots of practice. Yet it was worth the hard work.

Ann passed away quite suddenly a few years later. This sudden death caused me to have to process some real, grown-up emotions for the first time without my childhood rules. It's always a bit painful to look back and see the things we've missed and cannot recover; people we've lost, things we've messed up, and bridges we've burned. These circumstantial or accidental wounds might not have happened by choice. Ann helped me realize we do have a choice in how we respond. I can choose the meaning I assign to the things I can't control. Instead of ignoring them, as I did as a child, I now know I have the power to choose my emotional state.

I can start each day, approach each situation, and hear each conversation expecting something amazing. I am not afraid of expectations anymore, or the disappointments they offer. I know they also offer something amazing. I haven't ever gotten a tattoo, but I did paint this on my bedroom wall recently: EXPECT SOMETHING AMAZING! I love it!

When I decided my childhood rule didn't fit anymore, it was because I wanted something more. I didn't know I could reach for something amazing then, I sure do now. I believe you are reading this book because you want something different, something more, in some area of your life or ministry. It might not be clear yet, but I believe I have built that bridge for you in the pages of this book. I believe no matter where you are, or where you want to be, this bridge can take you there.

Please accept this as my personalized invitation to you, drawing from the language of my favorite poem, *The Bridge Builder*, "I have crossed the chasm deep and wide; I now build you a bridge at evening tide."

Will you cross with me?

It's going to be AMAZING!

I promise.

Chapter 1

Winter in the Midwest

Christmas Movies

It was winter in the Midwest (Omaha, to be exact). The trees were barren and the wind icy. The sun set a good hour before she got off work, and then there was the isolated commute home. It was not isolated because hers was the only vehicle on the road, but because she didn't notice the others. It was just another winter weeknight.

Arriving home, more numb than exhausted, she prepared a bag of popcorn and nested into her favorite spot on the sofa. She sat for a while in silence before turning on the television, just waiting. She looked at her cell phone, sitting ready near her, but it didn't ring. Of course it didn't; there was no one to call her. Everyone had their own things going on, their own set of circumstances to muddle through, or their own spouse to fight with . . . she didn't even have that anymore. He was gone. She thought about all the times when he was alive, after they'd been fighting and were both angry, that she'd wished he . . . well, she hadn't literally wished he was dead, had she? Maybe a few times, but she didn't give herself permission to expand on that. But now it was all she could do to not want to be dead herself. No one knew how lonely her life had become. She was sick of feeling closer to the characters in movies than real people. She was sick of wanting to go to sleep instead of wanting to wake up. She wasn't suicidal; she didn't want to die, but she was sick of being alive. She was tired of this life, sick and tired of this life . . . and it wasn't so much that no one else was aware of these things; the truth was *she* was not aware of them.

She had the remote control in one hand and a bag of popcorn in the other when she saw him. At first, he reminded her a bit of her father who had passed away when she was only a teenager. He stood, small and frail, in the corner of the room, just watching her curiously. She wasn't afraid, and she wondered about that later. Maybe it was a dream. She'd fallen asleep in front of a Christmas movie more times than she could count, and not just at Christmas time.

She looked again and caught his eye. After a moment, he subtly squeezed his arms together at his waist . . . then vanished. She breathed deeply, yet still she was not afraid. She closed her eyes to ponder it, and that is when she heard him.

"Bridge the gap," the little man said in a gentle, affectionate whisper. "Bridge the gap, my dear."

Writing it down seemed the sane thing to do, she thought, but with nothing particularly handy for writing, she simply opened her eyes and stared blankly at the corner where he'd been.

She'd never been very good at journaling. She loved a nice new journal, the way it smelled and felt; especially the potential it seemed to hold. She'd started many with a New Year's gusto, but the energy never lasted long. *Really,* she'd begun to think, *what is the point?* No one else would ever read it. She knew she wouldn't even re-read it. And, even though she was proud of her deep faith, she didn't write down prayers like some people were so faithful in doing. She didn't see the point of that either. If God actually needed her to pray, then He wasn't big enough for her to pray to, now was He? Her doubt and rationale never kept her from believing, but it didn't make much sense to log prayers to God when she believed Him to be sovereign enough to know her thoughts before she prayed them.

So journals rested unfinished in drawers, reminders of her own started life — started, shared, occasionally inspired, but now losing steam by each movie-infused night. Like a junkie who lived for that next fix, she would go through her day, and then return to this spot on the end of the couch, with her feet up and her choice of recorded, predictably romantic and idealistic Christmas movies cued up and playing into the night.

She thought about pulling a used journal from her stack of half-written ones right now. She knew exactly where they were. While she thought about it, and wondered if what had just happened had indeed just happened, she drifted off to sleep. The scenes from the television movie covered up all traces of the odd vision like a new fallen snow.

The next time she saw him was through the kitchen window as she sat with steaming coffee several mornings later. She immediately remembered their previous introduction. The little man walked with a bit of age, not too fast and not too slow. He walked all around the back yard as if checking the quality of the workmanship of the wooden privacy fence, and then he paused to look right at her. He smiled warmly; if he hadn't been so small and frail, she might have believed him to be St. Nick. As she contrasted the two characters in her mind, she noticed that the little man subtly touched both elbows to his waist and then vanished again.

Several seconds passed before she noticed she was holding her breath and finally let it out. Immediately when fresh oxygen filled her lungs, she thought about the journals. "Bridge the gap, my dear," the little man's voice spoke internally this time. "Bridge the gap." She rinsed her coffee cup and left for work.

She had almost reached retirement age. She'd always worked hard and consistently for large corporations with a retirement plan, but several times during her husband's cancer treatment years she'd had to borrow against those funds. So, although she didn't have to worry about having money for retirement, it wasn't enough to allow her to dream about a new life. She wondered sometimes what she would do all day after retirement. She wouldn't want to be around too many people, or be obligated to things, but she also didn't want to end up a hermit. She didn't think about it much more than that. Today she had to work, and that was that.

After work that day she stopped at a Hallmark store for cards. She did this routinely several times a year to buy cards for loved ones across the country, and now the world; her niece was stationed in Germany with the Air Force.

People rarely sent actual cards anymore, she always thought, so it had become a bit of a personal trademark to send them. It might well be the end of the world when her loved ones didn't get a card with a stamp delivered through the good old post office for their birthday, anniversary, or any other card occasion she happened to find the energy to shop for. She loved this card store. No one bothered her as she read cards and thought of those they fit perfectly.

That day, as if placed just for her as she checked out, was an attractive blue leather journal misplaced in the Christmas clearance bin, with a large cross embossed on the cover.

She stared at the cross just long enough to lose her focus for a moment, and in that moment, instead of a cross she saw a little bridge. "Bridge the gap," she remembered hearing.

She purchased three birthday cards, the blue journal, and a new pencil.

Chapter 2

Coming into Spring

After a full month, she'd only written in the blue journal a dozen times. She liked the pencil. She felt creative and playful with a pencil instead of a pen, and she wondered why she'd never thought of it before. She didn't know what to make of her hallucinations, although she pondered them each time she sat to write. She piddled with the journal, mostly sketching bridges and crosses, or an occasional snowman or snowflake . . . nothing fancy. She started paying attention to inspirational lines in her movies or meaningful lyrics from a song on the radio station during her commute. She'd write down the ones that stayed with her. Some of them made her cry as she wrote them, puzzling her slightly. She began to note the things that caused her to tear up, things that rang a chord of melancholy, sparked appreciation, or ignited a twinge of joy.

Valentine's Day came and went; she sent more than her usual amount of wishes. She didn't just mail cards this year, but also experimented with various forms of social media. She didn't mind these popular platforms, but was careful to only use them for intentional purposes such as this. She was far too practical to get all tangled in the drama of the masses and wanted to refrain from liking or friend-ing anyone who might misinterpret her lack of participation as lack of support.

She didn't receive any Valentine cards herself, but she knew how it would feel if she did, so she mailed them faithfully to her children, their spouses, ex-spouses and grandchildren, just as she'd always done.

Several weeks into March, he showed up again as she was trying to find a way to get the lawn mower from her garage into her husband's old truck. His hands were weathered, calloused and strong. He stepped in to pick up the other side of the awkward load, allowing her to slip it into the back of the bed with relative ease. She had to take it to get the blade sharpened. It was one of those chores her husband used to do himself, taking far too much time and effort than it was worth for very little benefit. She was going to pay for it to be done professionally, then she planned to learn to cut the grass herself this year, if nothing else just for the health benefits of being in the fresh air.

She closed the tailgate and hooked the latch her husband had hand-welded for this purpose (after the original factory latch had given way). She wondered if he would stay this time, the little man, since he'd gotten so close and been so helpful just now when she needed friendly assistance. She still was not at all afraid of his coming and going, but she was increasingly interested after this third encounter.

"I bought a journal," she began cautiously, expecting to engage him in a bit of friendly banter. She realized as she spoke how much she missed telling someone this small detail.

He smiled at her, his left eye twinkling a bit more than his right as he cocked his head and raised his chin ever so slightly. But he didn't reply as she'd hoped. Instead, he stepped backward, reached his arms wide and high above his shoulders as if funneling the dank air of the garage straight into his chest. She watched him blankly. Then he slowly returned his arms to his sides, touched his elbows to his waist, and disappeared.

This time she was not as complacent as before and said aloud, "Now wait just a minute! Who are you?" Then she immediately regretted that scolding tone and recanted gently, "Sorry, I'm just so appreciative and I'd like you to stay a bit longer next time . . . " Her voice trailed off as she realized a young boy and his mother were walking their golden retriever on the sidewalk past her house. The neighborhood threesome left sloppy wet tracks from the melting snow as they continued past her house and down the sidewalk. The tracks evaporated quickly in the direct sunlight, just as quickly as the little man had come and gone again. But then his voice characteristically followed. "Embrace it all, my dear," he said this time. "Embrace it all."

She decided to reschedule the mower drop-off until later in the week and spent the next hour pondering, wondering, questioning her sanity, and above all of that anticipating their next encounter.

Several days later she stopped to browse the clearance rack in the card shop and possibly end up with some half-priced Valentine's chocolates. St. Patrick's Day items had made their appearance overnight it seemed, and the Easter things were on brilliant display. She relished the idea that spring was nearly here.

In the religious/inspiration section, a misplaced card stood out. She could almost see the entire front of the card where it was perched oddly, returned by a previous patron in a hurry, she assumed. Against a pastel and grey cloudy sky, she recognized the distinct silhouette of a farmer raising his hands to the sky, arms spread wide above his head. Large drops of rain fell on his upturned face, closed eyes, and on his half-grown crops.

"Thank God . . . " it read on the front.

She stood, strangely frozen at the sight of it, for it resembled exactly the posture she'd seen the little man take in her garage. She almost reached for the card. But instead, she turned away abruptly and left without even glancing at the clearance chocolates.

Something didn't seem right all of a sudden and she wanted to be home. An hour later, she was choosing a movie, sipping a cup of very hot tea, and opening a bag of chips that would be gone before the movie was half finished. She didn't want to see him again, and she didn't ever want to write in a journal again. She didn't want to feel better. She didn't want to feel different. She just wanted to eat her chips and watch her movie. She kept herself from glancing at the corner of the room while she watched. Thirty minutes later the chips were gone, the tea was cold, and she had fallen asleep.

Her journal sat untouched until mid-April, a few days before Easter. When she stopped at the card shop that Thursday after work Jim, the regular clerk, recognized her and smiled but didn't call her by name or bother her as she browsed. Jim knew the repeat customers well and assumed assistance wasn't necessary today. She headed straight for the inspirational cards. But after twenty minutes of unusually frenzied searching, Jim could tell something was out of the ordinary. He was eventually asked for assistance, and was gracious in providing it. Unfortunately, Jim had to admit he was unfamiliar with the thankful-farmer-in-the-rain card. As a consolation, he ushered her to a new section of thank you cards near the front of the store. Here, all manner of artistic and poetic license converged to express spring-time gratitude and appreciation. But none of these cards were what she wanted.

What she wanted was to rewind. She wanted to go back to the way she'd felt a month ago, before she'd been here and seen the farmer-in-the-rain thank you card, before she'd freaked out and fallen into a funk.

She did not understand herself, and she certainly didn't understand the little man. And to be frank with herself and any spiritual presence concerned, she was beginning to question God's hand in messing with her mind like this. What had happened to her God of Peace, Love, and Solitude — her faithful movie and popcorn companion God? Why hadn't He seen fit to simply let her be? He had to be in on this madness.

She determined she would stay in this store until she found that card, no matter if she had to pick up and read every last bi-folded or tri-folded . . . *wait*. There it was! It was out of place in the clearance bin, right where the blue journal had been. She was immediately tempted to turn and leave without it again, thinking its placement was just too cliché. She didn't want to feel this out of control, she didn't want to be a pawn in some universal chess game. She desperately wanted . . . Well, she didn't actually know what she wanted.

She bought the card without so much as opening it to read what was inside. Then, as if she was afraid of some bad news, she waited another thirty minutes after she'd arrived home. She'd eaten a small snack and was fully ready for bed before she sat down to read what was inside the farmer card.

Thank God . . . She read on the front. And then she slowly opened to reveal the remainder of the message, " . . . *for everything.*"

Like a soft fleecy blanket wrapping around a scared child, the little man's words came back to her, "Embrace it all, my dear. Embrace it all." Her hands shook a little as she set the card down beside her bed. Holding back a sob as it threatened to shake her whole body, she gathered her own fleece blanket tightly around her and let the tears slip down her cheeks onto her pillow. After a few moments, she slept deeply.

He appeared in her dreams for the first time that night. She awoke so full of deep joy and gratitude, she forgot it was Good Friday. Absentmindedly, she got all ready for work before remembering she didn't have to leave the house that day. *No time like the present.* She decided it was time to pick up the journal again to write about the things she was grateful for — ALL the things. She began to write and again was impressed with how much she loved touching and using the pencil. She identified the obvious tangibles first: food, a job, a house, a car, etc. She explored the good and the perceivably bad, determined she would learn to embrace it all. It was a start. Another start.

She wished she could remember the dreams from the night before, but try as she might nothing came into clear focus. There was something uplifting about knowing he was in them, and she documented her gratefulness for that, too. She had gone to bed comforted and awakened inspired and encouraged. She was grateful for this special Easter experience.

She called her sons on Easter Sunday and shared He is Risen greetings with her grandchildren who replied with individual and varying levels of enthusiasm, "He is risen indeed, Grandma!" It was a highlight of her year to repeat this tradition. She marveled at the number of people in her neighborhood who did not attend church on Easter anymore. She didn't go for different reasons, she rationalized, but all those families with young children certainly should go.

As was her tradition each year on this day, she planned to surprise someone with a little Easter sunshine. She bought an Easter lily at the grocery store that afternoon and decided to take it to the family across the street. She'd never seen them leave the house on a Sunday morning and she thought it couldn't hurt. No one answered the door, so she left it on the front step, the sunshine reflected in all directions from the purple foil-covered pot as she walked away.

She wrote in her journal faithfully until June, never missing a day. *This*, she thought, *is the most committed I've ever been to journaling.* She even used a pen one day when her pencil broke and she didn't want to break her train of thought to sharpen it. It didn't bother her that half of the entry was in pencil and half was in pen.

She was happy she was writing; she was happy about a lot of things actually. Not that she had anyone to share them with, however she was beginning to want that again. She wanted someone to share in the joy. As she wrote that day, not only did she become aware that she deeply wanted someone to share her joy, but she also became aware of the fact that she was actually feeling joyful for the first time in a very long time.

Chapter 3

Five Years Later

The Conference

Five years after she'd purchased it, the blue
leather journal was long since filled. It was losing its
luster a bit, but certainly not its value. She caressed it
gently as she removed it from her suitcase and placed it
on the coffee table in a hotel suite. It always went with
her as a memento of her previous life and a reminder of
where life took its turn. She would take it with her to
the conference tomorrow morning and hold it up to the
audience when she shared her story. This was her life
now, she affirmed, far removed in so many aspects
from those early pages, but all the better for it, too, she
reflected.

Even though this was far from her first
experience at these conferences, she was still amazed at
the full-blown mix of excitement and anxiety. After the
first day of sessions attended by hundreds of women
and a few men, she poised herself for the meet-and-
greet and book-signing portion of the evening. She put

the journal away in her bag and hoped she'd inspired others to begin their own new life in the pages of their own journals. She was overcome with gratitude for the transformational journey hers had launched.

As members from the audience lined up to thank her in person for their inspiration, she wished she also had someone to thank in person for her own transformation. It would be nice to have a tangible hand to shake, or someone to capture in a photo to take home to enjoy in the morning solitude in her empty home. That part of her life had not changed. She still watched her Christmas movies year-round. She was still very lonely at times. She still mowed her own grass. She still didn't have many friends or social outings. But she'd never seen the little man again; he'd never appeared again after that day in the garage.

She had so longed for another sighting, but it hadn't stopped her transformation. It hadn't kept her from exploring herself through her journaling; she'd never wavered. Every now and again, he'd shown up in a dream, and a few times she was sure he'd left her some clue, a bit of wisdom or direction in or around her journal. She paused to think about some of those mysterious things briefly, but it wasn't long before she was back in the moment.

A young man had been waiting ever so patiently in the back of the convention hall, eyeing her as she signed books, took pictures, and visited with individuals and couples who'd been touched by her words. He finally saw his opening and approached the table.

He stayed a little more than an arm's length away. She looked up, awakened from reminiscing, and caught his eye. She was immediately drawn to him with a deep sense of compassion that was becoming more and more common for her. His nametag read Morgan. He spoke timidly, "I really shouldn't be here, I don't think," he began, nodding his head toward all the women who were slowly exiting the large room, "but I was so compelled to come."

She responded with her routine poise and grace, immediately stepping forward a bit to shake his hand. He seemed so nervous about being seen speaking to her, and she was instantly filled with a desire to dispel this anxiety. The lines of people were all but gone now, the other speakers were getting ready to head back to their respective rooms for the night. She asked Morgan if he'd like to sit down at a nearby dining table. He sighed with relief and sank weakly into the closest chair. She gathered her last few things and then affirmed with a member of the event staff that she was fine, safe, and needed no further help tonight. Then she took the chair exactly opposite of the young man.

She smiled warmly at him and tapped his hand. He seemed awfully thin for a man who looked to be only about 25 or so. She wondered what his anxieties were, but knew if it was relevant he'd bring it up shortly. He sighed and his eyes met hers briefly before he looked away again. She allowed him a minute to collect himself.

He finally commented about her story in the book and how much he'd enjoyed it, and then mentioned that his mom would have liked to meet her, if she could have come this weekend. She immediately offered to sign a book for his mother, but he declined. She was in very poor health, he explained, and she wouldn't be able to read it. He then spoke of how he'd read the book aloud to her recently and she'd encouraged him to come to the conference.

He stalled again, breathing shallowly; she wondered if his hesitancy to speak was due to physical or emotional limitations. She was patient, remembering her own anxiety from long ago, and felt great empathy for him. What was it he wanted, really? Assurance? Inspiration? Personal prayer? Encouragement? She waited.

"I don't understand the first key you speak of," he finally said with soft deliberateness. "How can self-awareness be so powerful?" He paused, and she knew he wasn't finished. "It doesn't change anything, really," he continued. "How can simply being more aware of what you *feel* make the transformational difference you speak of?" His voice and his eye contact seemed to fade into the vast emptiness of the conference room. It seemed difficult for him to swallow, he rubbed his finger on his knee in short little strokes as he formed one more sentence. "I guess I just struggle with doubt," he explained. "I don't doubt your story or those of the other speakers this weekend, but I doubt . . . if any of it can make a difference for me. Does that make sense?"

Oh yes, it did make sense. Self-doubt was one of the biggest roadblocks her readers spoke to her about, and was one of the areas she still had to address the most often in her current journaling. But she knew what to tell him. "Almost everyone I speak to, Morgan, thinks their circumstance is an exception at first," she assured him. "Don't worry about your doubts. It's actually a good thing when you are aware of it and you acknowledge it. If you have the capacity for doubt, you have the capacity for faith, too."

He took a deep breath and sighed. It was *emotional capacity* he remembered from the book. He nodded in appreciation and understanding. She was pleased she'd explained it in such a way as to bring him peace of mind.

Morgan continued to visit for another ten minutes or so, telling her that his mother was dying of a painful disease and that her only wish was to know how to make things right before she died, which appeared to be coming upon her soon. She had lived her life hating her late husband for many years of physical and emotional abuse. He'd apparently died in some sort of alcohol-related accident a few months prior to Morgan's birth. In the past year, his mother had come to trust in God again, Morgan explained with certainty, but she still had trouble letting the past go and enjoying what was left of her life.

Morgan described his mother as a very isolated, bitter and angry woman, but said when he'd read the book of life transformational stories to her a few weeks ago, she had seemed genuinely moved. A visible change happened in her. He said his mother seemed happier now than she'd ever been, more at peace somehow. When he'd mentioned the conference to her, she had insisted he take time away from her care and attend.

Ministry

She listened graciously until he finished his story and thanked her again. He then picked up his notebook as she gathered her bag. This would go into her memory as yet another meaningful connection to validate she was doing the Lord's work in her retirement years. She would sleep in peaceful assurance tonight. *Well done, good and faithful servant.* She smiled and touched his hand, preparing to offer to pray for him and wish him well.

But then, as if she'd already left the room in spirit, she was sucked back into the present moment with a jolt.

"Would you consider staying in touch?" he asked. "Maybe to work with me personally as I start journaling and attempt my own transformational journey?"

She froze. Every neuron in her brain came to full attention as if bracing for attack; her heart raced, and her mouth went dry. Morgan had asked one simple question, but it screamed out with all the emotional equivalency of a civil defense siren alerting all nearby residents to a tornado sighting. It wasn't a horribly inappropriate request, she told herself, but she had trouble calming.

Could he stay in touch and work with her during his own transformation after this weekend was complete? Could he continue to work with her . . . work with her . . . work with . . . with her . . . It seemed to echo around in her brain.

"I'm sorry if that was too forward," he tried to adjust to her flattened expression. "You usually only minister to women, don't you?"

He had no idea that she didn't see herself ministering to anyone at all. She'd given up ministering to people many decades and two husbands ago. It was all so long ago she was barely able to remember the face of the timid woman she had been then! But, she vividly — too vividly, apparently — remembered how it felt.

She'd traded her former self in for a newer, shinier model since then. She'd moved away. She'd chosen a real life in the private sector. She'd remarried a nice man, and she had not even so much as darkened the doors of a church again until this retirement roadshow gig had presented itself.

She knew she was okay with God; that had never been in question. But, ministry? No. Ministry was a completely different thing. It made her squirm so strangely inside she could not excuse herself fast enough to get back to her room — to her journal. She knew what to do, and she knew she needed to do it quickly.

She saw Morgan's sad eyes the entire walk back to her room. She would meet him the next day for breakfast, she had promised that, and she had told him where to find her. She was very tired from the travel, she'd explained graciously. But, his eyes! They seemed to plead with her, staying with her: frightened, desperate, hungry eyes. They went with her, quickening a part of her she'd long since put away.

She didn't want to think of all this as being in ministry again, but her eyes filled with tears as she remembered touching his hand. She wished she'd been able to say aloud to him, "Of course, Morgan. Of course we can keep in touch and I'll work with you and your dying mother. We'll keep in touch as much as you'd like." But she hadn't said that and she didn't think she could say it with sincerity even now or at the upcoming breakfast.

He thought she could coach him through a life transformation like she'd experienced. Telling her story was fine. She could talk about how journaling had transformed her life and she loved when that story inspired others. But these were real people, looking to her for real answers, and asking her for those answers while they stood before her in real pain. These weren't just people in an audience she'd only see once and never meet again.

She didn't know what to do. She had done the work in her own life to bring herself out of isolation, to get through her husband's death, to move from numbness to joy, and to move from isolation back into relationships and into what some would even consider to be success as she toured with this group and shared her testimony. She had a good friend now. She could enjoy life. She was happy!

She thought back to those very lonely years and she stroked her blue journal as she set it on the nightstand in her room. As she did so, she heard the little man's voice in her heart almost audible as always, "Bridge the gap, my dear. You can do it. Bridge the gap."

As many times as she'd heard that phrase, and as life-changing as the journey had been since that first time, it had never seemed as confusing as it did right now. Why now, after all these years would she be confused by it? What was there to be confused about? She sat immediately, as had become her habit, and flipped to the closest empty page in her current journal and began with her routine prompt:

"What is it I see, hear, feel, know, or believe about myself or this situation right now?" She then began to flood those answers onto the page:

Fear, confusion, inadequacy, faith, love, service, opportunity . . . The mismatched list of random emotions and observations continued for a few minutes until she filled the page. Then she stood, raised her hands above her head and said aloud the things she wished to release from herself and her situation, followed by those she was choosing to draw strength from and keep close. She prayed aloud, yet softly, to conclude her time, identifying with a heart of compassion, service, and openness to the work of the Holy Spirit. The fear was gone; she was overflowing with gratitude.

Knowing her next step was to take action from this empowered emotional state, she walked to the hotel lobby and asked the front desk clerk if there might be somewhere close by she could buy a greeting card. About a block away was an all-night pharmacy, he explained, and they would probably have something like that. She pulled her summer sweater a bit tighter around her as she slipped out quickly into the night air. Morgan's mother would get a card with a personal note, even though she wasn't sure yet what that note would say.

Chapter 4

The Model

All models are imperfect,
but some are extraordinarily helpful.

Perfect Timing

An hour later she sat to write at her hotel desk, the clock on the nightstand reading almost midnight. She didn't care about the time right now, but ordinarily she was asleep long before this. She realized she'd not gotten the woman's name so she addressed the card

To Morgan and his dear Mother

Her hands trembled a little as she waited, as if for direction, with the pen in mid-stream.

And then — there he was!

It was first time she'd seen him outside of a dream in a little over four years. She didn't really know if she was dreaming now but was so happy to have him presenting himself at such a crucial point, she shrieked a little with delight and stood up so fast the chair almost tipped over.

"Oh my! Hello." She greeted him, and he smiled as always, looking right through her like honey. He stood next to the window across the sitting area from her. She moved toward him a little and held up the card and pen.

"What should I say to them?" she asked. "I don't know what they need from me."

His eyes twinkled and his arm moved slightly at the elbow. "No!" she reached out her hand toward him trying to keep her volume low. She didn't want him to vanish just yet. "Please, stay a bit."

He did.

She let her breath go and moved to sit on the couch facing him.

He was distant yet close, spirit yet human, and she wondered if he was actually someone she'd known.

Was he her husband? She didn't even believe in that type of thing so she didn't know why it crossed her mind.

Was he a picture of herself somehow?

Was he Jesus?

Was he an angel?

Was he someone else from her past or her future? All these thoughts rushed around in her mind, but she spoke none of them.

He raised his eyebrows a bit and nodded, as if it was okay to ask him something. Feeling encouraged to speak, she couldn't even think of what to ask now. "What should I tell them?" she heard herself repeating.

His eyes were so warm and deep; they exuded all the love she'd ever felt in her life all in one place. He tipped his chin up and smiled so cheerfully, as if chuckling out loud. She imitated him and actually chuckled aloud with joy. He did so remind her of the men who played the Santa roles in the Christmas movies she still loved so much. He raised his hand and tapped his fingers on his heart, and then before she could say anything more, he touched his elbows softly to his belt and disappeared.

She stroked her hands together, waiting for his words. They had always come plainly after his vanishing . . . and they came like sweet dessert, "Go within, my dear. Go within or you'll go without."

She sat there for a long time before moving back to the desk. So long in fact, that after she'd finally finished writing a few words on the greeting card and climbed into bed, the clock displayed 1:37a.m. She'd not been truly happy with her sentiments on the card, but she decided she'd see what she thought of her message in the morning. The card said started with, "Thinking of you at this difficult time," and the only thing she'd been able to write in addition to that had seemed so trite.

"Go within or go without," he'd just told her. What did that mean? Why did he always have to be so mysterious? She wasn't actually bothered by it; she was so grateful for the nugget to chew on as she slipped off to sleep.

The next morning she read her message on the card:

I'll be praying for you both as you maneuver through this time. I pray joy and peace over you, and will be praying you'll find joy in your hope for the future. Eternal life is promised to those who believe. We can move from this life to the next knowing fully that we are His.

She felt peace with it. She decided it exactly reflected her heart, and that is precisely what he had meant when he gestured to her, tapping his hand on his heart, before he disappeared.

She pondered what the little man had said and attempted to put it all together with her confusion from the day before. *Bridge the gap. Embrace it all. Go within or go without.* How did they go together? How did this fit with her hesitancy to enter back into what felt like ministry? She didn't know, but she trusted that it would become clear if she stayed in integrity and continued to move forward in faith.

She scanned the breakfast room for Morgan and eventually saw him. She was able to give him the card and a hug, and then felt she should give him the message from the little man, too. She urged him to tell his mother to go within —or go without, and even as she spoke those words, she wished she understood fully what they meant. She would ponder them, and she was certain they would eventually make sense on the pages of her journal; this is how it always went. That is where things became clear. That is how it worked.

The Model

She didn't want to stay for the rest of the conference speakers that day, as she usually did. She felt tired from the short night so she retreated to her room for a nap part way through the morning session. When she arrived back in the room, she immediately sensed something familiar and sure enough; he was there. What a pleasant surprise! Two days in a row, and this time he was sitting. She sat too. "You know," she began, "I'm curious about your words last night."

He'd never spoken directly to her; she'd only heard his words after, but still she wanted to see if he would.

He reached out toward the coffee table between them and pushed her blue journal toward her. A pencil marked a page near the very end. He must have placed it there. She opened to it. Several times in those first years of her journaling adventure, the little man would mark pages like this in her journal. One morning she woke to find he'd sketched something for her. The page marked now was that very one.

The sketch was a large V taking up the entire page from the top corners to the bottom center. The inside space of the V was separated by a ladder running from the top of the page to the bottom, essentially separating the V into two halves, perfectly symmetrical. He'd labeled the ladder Authenticity and he had written Embrace Emotional Capacity across the top of the page. This was the day she decided to affectionately call him her Bridge Builder, because of his first words to her and because his words across the top of the model seemed like a little bridge from left to right. She'd never told anyone about him —not a soul! Who would understand? Still, she thought he needed some sort of name, even if it was never spoken aloud.

This page in the blue journal had become a roadmap of sorts. She had looked at the little sketch often and judged many things against it. She'd come to know it almost as well as anything she'd written herself. Over the next few years, it became the model that explained herself, her emotions, her reactions, her motivations, and it had eventually led her here. At one time, it was the only thing that had helped her find courage when she felt afraid, the thing that helped her feel excitement instead of nervousness when she spoke at the conferences, and what helped her resist the old familiar mindsets of isolation and numbness. When life seemed to want more of her than she felt ready for, she would return to the model to find inspiration. Yet, as strangely helpful as it had been, she'd never actually shared it — the model — as an integral part of her transformation story.

As she stared at the sketch again now, she realized she'd gotten away from it somehow. She had not thought of it once last night as she battled the anxiety of the ministry opportunity. It was the entire basis for the principle of *emotional capacity*, the concept Morgan understood from her story. If he had the capacity for doubt, he knew he had the capacity for faith; that was one of the lessons she'd learned from exploring this model. She'd gotten comfortable with the fact that it had helped her in the beginning; now she knew she'd taken it for granted.

Do you want me to share this? She looked up to ask him, but he wasn't there anymore.

She waited, eyes closed, pencil in hand, waiting.

Soon, he spoke. "Look to the space, my dear; therein lies your freedom."

She scribbled it quickly along the corner of the well-worn page where the V was first drawn.

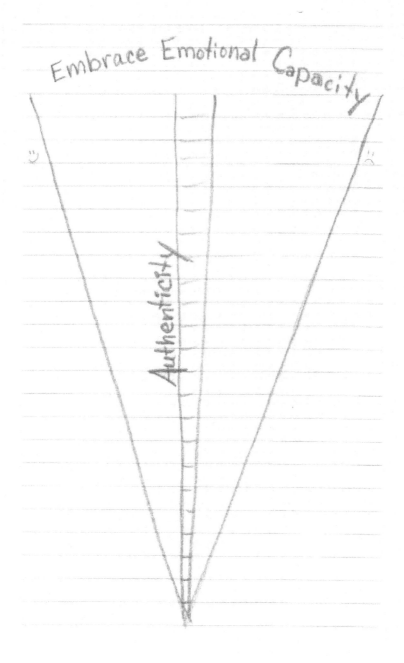

Embrace Emotional Capacity

Authenticity

She immediately remembered the question Morgan had asked the previous evening when they first met. "How can being aware make that much difference?" The Bridge Builder was here to remind her that it was not just awareness Morgan needed to understand. She knew she needed to explain the model in its entirety.

She sat then and scanned back over the other pages in that well-worn part of the journal and found some other things she'd almost forgotten. Personal Awareness of the Space she'd written on the next page. She'd underlined the P, the A, and the S. PAS: Personal Awareness of the Space.

She also remembered the quote that followed. She'd heard it on a podcast or something and written it here: "Between the stimulus and the response, there is a space. Therein lies your freedom."

"Look to the space," he had just encouraged her, " . . . therein lies your freedom." The space was another key she'd gotten away from. It was the bridge for the gap, the bridge to freedom. This was the place to begin her new level of authenticity — her new step into ministry.

All the pieces connected like a jigsaw puzzle and it made more sense when she put it all together. *Bridge the gap. Embrace it all. Go within. Look to the space.* She was pleased to see the pattern emerging. The bridge was building itself. She didn't have to worry about connecting the pieces.

She grabbed her pencil and drew a little stick man standing in the V with his hands raised to bridge the gap from left to right. Personal awareness of the space, authenticity, embracing it all, going within — these were all keys to the model, keys to transforming one's life with new ways of thinking — and she knew she had a mentee poised and ready to learn it, if she was ready to minister.

She decided then and there to work with Morgan over the next six months. She felt nervous thinking about it, but she knew she could reframe it as excitement. It seemed amazing, and scary, and nothing short of stunning to think of the vast amount of insight she had stepped into in the past 48 hours, the past five years, since the Bridge Builder had first appeared.

She now wanted that nap she'd come to her room for an hour ago. She closed her eyes and took in the wonder and mystery of her life. She paused intentionally to give God her praise, her breath, her sheer and utter delight and gratitude.

The afternoon was a blur, but it always was on the final day of any event. She loved the activity and the busyness, and then she loved being back in her room alone, too. She was aware she was rushing back, just in case he was there again. When he wasn't she tried not to be too disappointed.

She just got ready for bed and then, of course, picked up her current journal. This journal was sure to become one of her favorites. Some just got put away when they were filled and were not looked at again. But this one was special. It had been a gift from her friend Sandra a few months ago on her birthday. The cover was bright with an ocean sunrise and in the foreground was a beautiful glittering starfish. The pages were tan and textured a little bit, like touching soft wet sand. Now it was even more special since she had written about seeing the Bridge Builder again in its pages.

With pencil in hand, the thoughts of getting back into ministry were flooding themselves out on the soft pages. Some of them were still downright frightening, but she was attempting to explore what was actually causing her fear. She felt safe doing these conferences with the other women, telling her story and signing books for people. She wasn't out of her comfort zone here with this group. But comfort zones didn't fit neatly into the emotional capacity model the Bridge Builder had given her. They were also not highly touted in scripture, so she knew she couldn't quench her thirst for security within their familiar spaces.

She was pretty sure if she'd known up-front that this author/speaker path would take her back into ministry, she would have backed away. She was certain if anyone had actually used the word "ministry" for the traveling work they were doing, she would have politely declined to participate. She might never have written this book with them at all. And, she might have even cursed the day the little man had showed up in her living room. *No*, she thought, *I know too much now to think that way.* She had become accustomed to this type of wide emotional ebb and flow, but it still surprised her sometimes how fast the waves could come and go, almost knocking her down. She recognized her heart's increasing capacity for the vast emotional opposites. She used to see them as conflicts and back away, but now that she knew her emotions were nothing to fear, she could more easily lean in to notice them. Like the starfish on the cover of her journal, she could handle them with care, explore them, name them, and appreciate their uniqueness and their value.

Because she knew the pattern of these waves and tides now, she knew she could expect something wonderful to happen next. This was the concept of emotional capacity — it was just waiting for her to embrace it all, and bridge the gap. It was just as she'd explained to Morgan when they first met; if he had the capacity for doubt, he also had the capacity for faith.

Chapter 5

The Ministry Box

After a full soft, sandy page of processing everything she could find in her current personal space that night, she set down her journal. Before this weekend, she'd mistakenly assumed she'd reached the pinnacle of her own transformational journey. As she drifted off to sleep she was consciously aware that her transformation was not like that of a butterfly emerging from a cocoon. It was not something to be completed; it was to be a lifelong work.

Her conscious processing had concluded peacefully for the day, but her subconscious didn't seek sleep yet; a few more things still wanted to be acknowledged, and they tugged at her from a place deep inside. They were deeper than her memories, deeper than her heart, deeper —several layers deeper. A sealed up box in the back of a hall closet was screaming to be opened, aired out, released, set free. She heard it, she saw it, she turned away from it but it pulled her back. It found its way from the closet. It was huge, worn, patched, smelly. It was marked with big black scribbled letters:

Ministry Years.

In her dream she was a pale, skinny, 23-year-old woman sick, burning up with fever, caring for herself and for two crying babies, all alone. She was utterly alone. The only other thing in the house with them was this disgusting old box. Slapping at her own hands to keep from it, she finally reached out to touch the gruesome box waiting in the recesses of her mind and then lifted the lid . . .

Expecting to be overwhelmed with something that didn't happen, she took an oversized pencil and began to inventory the contents of the box on a yellow pad. It went on for pages; she wanted to stop, but couldn't. She was compelled to empty the box. They were not books or shoes or tangible things, but heavy weighted blobs not easily identified, greyed and misshaped. When the list was completed, she began to flip each of the contents over and inventory the other half. This had worked before when she was awake, but she'd never opened a wound this deep by herself, dreaming or otherwise. She watched her younger self scribble furiously with the pencil to finish the list, inverting all the negatives to positives, all the painful emotions to more desirable ones:

On the other side of abandoned she'd written adopted, on the other side of betrayed was protected, on the other side of defeated was victorious. She also jotted down Bible verses that floated around in the air and song lyrics that mixed into the dream's sounds.

And then, when it was done, the woman she'd once been sat quietly on the floor next to the empty box, the babies content and her own body fully relaxed. The unacknowledged emotions that had been given names were now released to evaporate, floating far away into the night sky. There was no longer any place for them to be stored in her heart. The space was full instead with all the opposites, with authentic love, joy, and peace.

She awoke then.

It was a little before midnight and she felt complete peace.

Remembering much of the dream, she turned on a lamp. Picking up her pencil, she transcribed what she remembered from the lists in her dream into her starfish journal then pictured herself folding up an empty box marked **Ministry Years** to put it in the trashcan next to her bed.

She stood then, as she'd become accustomed to doing. This was the process she knew the little man came to give to her. She held her right hand up and unfolded her fingers to release all the undesirable emotions she'd listed. She then lifted her left hand, and in this hand she embraced all the opposite emotions: the more desirable, beneficial ones, the ones that agreed with the very heart of God. She stood quietly, allowing herself to simply notice the presence of God, His delight and favor, and the overwhelming gratitude and affection that flooded her being. She felt nothing but love at that moment. Love for God, for herself, for her life — her past, her present, and her future.

She thought of all those faces she'd looked at every Sunday when she and her first husband had led that tiny church flock so many years ago, and marveled that she'd never really seen them. In much the same way, she realized, she'd been speaking at these conferences with a group of women she barely knew, weekend after weekend, sharing meals and stories and plane trips together, without really ever seeing them.

And now she smiled, knowing the grace of God had used this dream not only for her own healing, but to launch her into an entirely new ministry to others.

his was to be ministry with a whole new blend of authenticity and energy.

No Wrong Way

When she met with Morgan before leaving the hotel that morning, he started with a string of questions. She laughed at how energetic and receptive he'd become. It was such a contrast to the timid soul who'd approached her only a few days before.

How, he wanted to know, did all this emotional awareness fit into his relationship with Jesus Christ? Wasn't his Christian life supposed to be one of submission and service, and not so focused on emotion? Was all this emotional mumbo jumbo just a distraction from what he was supposed to be doing with his life? Was he getting caught up in something that was only going to make it more difficult to properly grieve the death of his mother and "move on" with the rest of his life?

She responded to his questions with gentleness and encouragement.

She vividly remembered feeling the same sense of curiosity and confusion, but not having anyone to talk to about it, no one to ask. She told Morgan what this had been like for her to plod through some of this journey alone and she encouraged him to reach out to her as often as he felt the need. There was no reason to muddle through something alone, she assured him.

She turned to one of the pages in the old blue journal and showed him a sample of one of her early journaling attempts:

doubt, anger, disgust, annoyance, blackness, heaviness, faith, weakness, strength . . .

The list of mismatched emotions went on a bit and then she asked him to identify some of his own immediate emotions.

He did: *uncertainty, excitement, dread, heaviness, faith, helplessness, anticipation, hope.* They then found a few Bible verses to affirm the voice of the Holy Spirit in the midst of these emotions. One passage was from Romans 8:15-17. She assured him that she had come to know that God is a supremely emotional being. She challenged him to read his Bible with new awareness from then on, looking for the immense emotional capacity of God in its pages.

She left him with another challenge to think about on the drive home. Aren't each one of the fruits of the spirit (in Galatians, chapter 5) emotional states? She wasn't sure that concept would actually "preach" in church, she told him, but she thought it was a good perspective to chew on and wanted him to come to his own conclusions.

He wanted to know how to get started on his journaling before they got together again and she encouraged him to simply start by listing emotions in random order whenever he was aware of them. This was a technique she called flooding. Naming our emotions is a bit like naming our pets, she explained. What we own, at least in American culture, we give a special name.

"I know people who name their cars!" Morgan interjected. They laughed and then admitted they had both done this, too.

"If we have pets," she continued, "they follow us around in our personal space 24/7, and then further demand that we feed them and pay attention to them, just like emotions. They deserve to have names." But just like there are no real right or wrong ways to name things, she reminded him, there was really no right or wrong way to journal.

He laughed as if this thought of doing it right might have been holding him back a bit, and she suggested he try using a pencil if he was given to a perfectionist temperament like she'd once been. Again, his expression indicated she'd nailed the issue exactly; he raised both hands in mock surrender.

"Journaling our emotions and increasing our awareness and authenticity doesn't change the situation or the circumstances. But it subtly changes us in those situations. It allows us to be our best selves in the circumstances that present. It is really just a vehicle that helps you get where you want to go."

"Just remember," she reminded him again, "There's no wrong way to journal."

Chapter 6

Authenticity

Father's Day

Morgan called her two weeks after the conference. She missed his call while she was buying Father's Day cards for her sons. She'd thought about him while she was browsing the cards, wondering if Father's Day was ever difficult for him. He'd not had a chance to know anything about his father outside his mother's hate for the man.

After listening to the voicemail, she returned his call from the car just before she drove home from the card store. He explained that his mother had passed a few nights after he'd arrived home from the conference. He said everything was taken care of now and he was ready to move forward. She offered her condolences and prayed with him, and then they set up their first official session for the following weekend. She'd be prayed up and ready, ready to minister with authenticity.

Authenticity is where her transformation had started before she knew what to call it. Her daughter-in-law had given her a copy of *Daring Greatly* by Brene Brown when she was still writing in her blue journal. She read it to be polite. She was immediately challenged to live her life more fully, more courageously, and she was intrigued by the concept of vulnerability even though she didn't fully embrace the term.

Vulnerability indicated a feeling of nakedness and she wasn't quite ready for that exposure with others. When the Bridge Builder labeled the ladder in the model Authenticity, it clicked! This term was just a better fit, a much more palatable word. As she explored the concept further throughout that next year, she came to see the similarities and the differences and these helped her *know* herself enough to *be* herself. She was certain that since this was where she'd begun, it was the perfect place to begin mentoring Morgan.

Mentoring, too, was a more palatable word, she decided, for this new ministry role. It was all about the emotional connotation, she told herself. Mentoring fit better, so she could be her most authentic self for the experience.

Preparing to Mentor

As she prepared to guide Morgan into his transformation, she spent some time remembering the day she'd first awakened to find the model in the blue journal.

She'd since come to call it the Emotional Capacity Model. Now she wondered if she should abbreviate that to ECM. *Hmmm . . .* She didn't know if that rolled off the tongue or not. Maybe she'd simply let Morgan decide if they should call it something else. Names seemed to come along in their own time. The Bridge Builder had stuck, so surely this would sort itself out too.

It had been early fall that first year when she'd awakened to find the large V. She remembered that because she was intentionally avoiding the card store's Halloween decorations and was instead adjusting to the shortening days by rushing home right after work to rake leaves. A bit emotionally and physically exhausted from this season, she'd left her journal open on the nightstand that night.

The delight she experienced finding the little man's sketch in the morning still thrilled her looking back. She had been excited beyond words knowing he'd been there, and was a bit giddy with expectancy that he might reappear. In that state of excitement, she'd grabbed sticky notes at work to sketch things and jot little connecting thoughts to take home to her journal. She had even run herself out of the little pink sticky notes she kept in her purse. The expectancy finally wore off, but the little notes had helped her compile her early skeleton understanding of the model. Those early days of understanding authenticity were quiet and gentle. Nowhere in the process did she feel exhausted. Nowhere in it did she feel overwhelmed. Nowhere did she feel that she just wanted to avoid or get away from her life by escaping into a movie. Instead, she actually enjoyed movies now. She no longer needed them to numb her or fill the boredom and complacency of her isolated existence.

She filled that original blue journal as October faded into November, and she was so glad for the timing; she wanted to stop at the card store to choose another.

Seasons Change

Right after she started her fresh journal (a distinctly patriotic design from the clearance bin), she'd received the news at work. This was a real-life test of authenticity. It was also a real opportunity to slip back into her former habits: she slept in, enjoyed the cooler weather, lit the artificial fire in the fireplace every evening, and began to record all the new Holiday/Christmas movies. Forced early retirement. She had not seen it coming.

She especially longed for the Bridge Builder to visit again with a new bit of wisdom, even in a dream. She sat many nights enjoying movies and popcorn, but he didn't show. She had to decide who she really was —with or without any additional wisdom. Did it matter if she received more valuable insights, or did it matter more that she lived out the valuable insights she already had? She knew the answer to that without journaling.

Being unexpectedly retired and all, she had filled that patriotic journal very quickly. She'd realized in its pages her sincere desire to cultivate a friendship. She wanted to share her authentic joy for life. It was hard to believe how calloused and isolated she'd been a short year ago, when the little man had showed up for the first time. She was now bursting with a desire for friendship.

She decided to start by reaching out to Sandra, the charming woman pastor who had officiated her husband's funeral. They were about the same age. Coincidentally, when they'd chatted at the grocery store a few days ago, Sandra had invited her to call anytime to get together for coffee. She so missed chatting with someone. Maybe it was the emerging Christmas atmosphere sparkling everywhere she looked, but she felt as if she would burst if she didn't find a way to share the joy that was bubbling up, overflowing from her heart.

For quite a while that first conversation with Sandra had centered on the holidays and its traditional calendar events. Then it moved easily to each woman's family members, and then how the weather would surely affect the upcoming Christmas pageants and people's travel plans. The conversation finally turned to give each woman a chance to be more vulnerable and authentic.

When Sandra asked more in depth questions, she was delighted to fully express how different she felt now, how transformed she was from a year ago. She shared with Sandra the journaling journey she had been traveling. Sandra, always thinking ministry, immediately wanted to collaborate about how the benefits of journaling like this could be duplicated in other women's lives. The two women decided to get together more often.

Over the next year, the two had become dear friends and met as regularly as Sandra's schedule would allow. One day Sandra called with an invitation. Would she please come to Sandra's church the following weekend and give her testimony at a ladies' brunch? The topic was "Spiritual growth through journaling." With nervousness in check, she chose to focus on her authentic heart and accepted the invitation.

Her authentic heart was feeling excitement, joy, peace, and a sincere love for others. Her heart, she was discovering, was one of encouragement and service, and the more she operated from that heart, the more authentic she was.

Lesson One: Awareness

Morgan called as planned for their first session. Since he lived a little over two hours away, they would do most of their work over the phone. It didn't take them long to get right down to business. He bought a journal and had already done quite a bit of work. He wanted to know more about her own experiences with grieving and she was glad she'd decided not to bring up fathers today. He was missing his mother.

For the first hour they simply talked about what he'd already processed since his mother's passing. Then they talked about how his journaling was progressing. She was impressed with his enthusiasm. He listened carefully as she told a little bit of her story with grief and how she came to understand the principles she was about to share with him.

She had him start by drawing a large V on his journal page and labeling the ladder up the center: Authenticity. She felt awkward when she first started to teach him, but he listened intently as she spoke and soon it became easier to find the right words. He paused her often to clarify and she could tell he was taking detailed notes.

She wasn't sure how much to give him at his first session, but after what seemed like a good portion of time she stopped and he summarized it back well.

- If I am unaware of my emotions, my authenticity is very low. This is not always isolation from other people, but it can look like that.
- When I move up and down on the ladder of authenticity, I am more or less tuned into my true emotional state.
- Being authentic requires me to increase my emotional awareness and my emotional vocabulary.
- Authenticity requires that I be clear and specific when naming my emotions. What I own, I name; what I name, I own; and what I own, cannot own me. I am then the master of my emotions.
- When I'm authentic, I control my emotional state, rather than it controlling me.
- Authenticity is not the same as vulnerability.

After this last point he paused. "So, do you think vulnerability is different because it is what other people can see —more of an outward, visible expression?" he half-stated and half-asked.

"I don't think I've ever even thought to say it that way, but, yes. Our authenticity is our best understanding of ourselves. We might present ourselves as brave and courageous, which could be seen as vulnerability. But we might not be acting authentically from our heart or in agreement with our core values," she offered.

He continued to explore his understanding. "It sounds like authenticity is how fully I know my motivations, my wiring, or my mindsets. It's internal if I'm flipping over outward, the word I used a minute ago."

"Yes, God knows our true selves at all times," she added. "He alone knows our hearts. This first part of my transformation was all about getting to know me as He knows me, and that's what you'll do first."

He commented that he had plenty to get started on and she encouraged him by assuring Morgan there was no hurry. "Don't forget to keep living your life," she urged him, knowing even as she said it how difficult that advice would have been for her to hear right after her husband's death.

The Fourth of July was upon them. He said he had a few friends who wanted him to attend their picnics and celebrations in the next few days, as well as the fireworks displays. He commented that he struggled knowing if he should be out enjoying himself and being happy so quickly after the funeral. Of course, she suggested he journal about these feelings and then act from there, authentically. If he was actually happy, he didn't need to feel bad about acting happy, because it was authentic and obviously his mother would want him to enjoy a happy life. He had to chuckle at the simplicity of this advice based on what they had just discussed.

Authentic Patriotism

They wrapped up their time together then by setting up another time to meet then praying together. As soon as she got off the phone, she immediately drove to the card store to choose a new patriotic flag for the front of the house. Fourth of July was something she'd never really decorated for before, but today she wanted to.

When she'd begun writing in her patriotic journal it was wintertime, but the red, white, and blue journal cover had triggered lots of summery emotions even then. Her late husband had been a veteran and so were both her sons. Now, two of her nephews and a niece were in the military. There was something very authentic about her sense of patriotism, she observed.

"Authenticity is the freedom of knowing oneself and then acting from that sincere knowledge," she said aloud to herself as she hung her new flag near the front porch. She made a mental note to write that down as soon as she went inside.

So here she was, still climbing in authenticity and continuing her own transformation. She intentionally breathed in this awareness and felt an abundance of gratitude for life, summer, and freedom. Whenever she savored gratitude like this, it was like putting on wings — and today they felt like the wings of a majestic bald eagle. A new level of authenticity was calling for her to fly, and she was answering.

Chapter 7

Emotional Capacity

No Rush

Morgan came to their next meeting in person. They sat on her back porch watching the rabbits eat some clover in her un-manicured lawn at the edge of town. It was an early August morning; the day would turn hot and humid quickly, but it was still pleasant at this time of morning. He had to come into the city to finalize a few legal things first thing this morning. The cemetery was close too, and he'd take care of all these errands after they met.

His grief was a major focus of his journaling the past month; it was a good backdrop to explore the concept of authenticity. He was finding more words for his feelings, she noticed, intentionally increasing his emotional vocabulary. As he shared with her, she was reminded of her own journeys through grief. She marveled at the ease with which he seemed to be maneuvering this one. He teared up a few times, and so did she. She was able to share a few of her own experiences, but mostly she just held space; listening to him, hearing him out, allowing him a safe place to be both vulnerable and authentic, brave and real.

She decided the next piece of the model could wait for next time. The ladder of authenticity was first for a reason. If she knew anything for sure, it was that no matter how uncomfortable it was, becoming keenly aware of one's present state was absolutely necessary to moving out of it into a more desirable one. As much as she wanted to rush Morgan through his grieving, she knew she shouldn't shortcut his process.

The Measure

Like lots of other things, the Bridge Builder had left her a clue to introduce the journaling technique she was now so anxious to teach Morgan. One morning she'd found her journaling laying open with two shiny quarters sitting on the blank page. She instantly knew he'd been there. She looked around and sat down for a bit, curious if he'd come back. He didn't, so she eventually picked up the quarters and examined them curiously. One was heads-up, the other was tails-up.

After she picked them up, she noticed h.
around each of them in pencil and then written lightr,
"*Which is more valuable?*" It was a silly, rhetorical
question, but she had long since quit thinking about
why he did things. Instead she'd decided to focus on
how the little appearances (or lack of them, in this case)
could be useful and helpful.

She always found that if she sat quietly for a bit,
a few words would come, almost audible but more in
her heart than her head. This time was no exception:
"You pick the measure, my dear." She loved how he
always called her that. No one else ever had, so it was
special. His familiar voice then repeated, "You pick the
measure."

She'd written this down beside the two circles
and his question. She then built upon it as she grew to
understand more about the concept of emotional
capacity. A measure was simply a fixed amount. When
she thought of it like money, she saw more than just
flipping it over to the other side and having the same
amount. She began to think of it more like doubling the
amount.

She pondered: if someone offered to double her
money she wouldn't give him a quarter to double, but

erything she could possibly hand over, including any $100 dollar bills she could find, without hesitation!

If it's a matter of expanding my capacity for all the opposite, wonderful things I want to experience and enjoy in life, then I'll want to open up the capacity as far as I can! she'd written later that day. She began to think outside the concept of money. *What other things can be flipped over or doubled? What about emotions?*

Soon after finding the quarters, her mind was expanding again when she chose to listen to a teaching by one of her favorite speakers, Graham Cooke. He suggested a new perspective on problems. His suggestion was to treat a problem like receiving a large package at the door. We answer the door, sign for it, and then drag it inside—with anticipation!

Then, recognizing this box contains a "problem," we call up a friend, giddy with excitement, before opening it, saying something like this: "If the problem is THIS BIG, how much bigger will the promise be?! God's really going to turn this around, right? COOL!"

He suggested that by God's design we must move to a different level in order to receive the promise on the other side of the problem. As the Bible says, "Counting it all joy." No problem, he insisted, is ever solved at the same level as it was received.

She knew the level he spoke of was what she'd come to know as authenticity, and the size of the problem represented emotional capacity. The Bridge Builder had told her she could choose the size of her emotional capacity when he told her, "You pick the measure, my dear." Coming slowly into the understanding of the concept of emotional capacity, then applying it in her life over the past few years was one thing. But finding a way to explain it to Morgan was yet another!

Encouragement Card

There were not any holidays to shop for over the next two weeks, there weren't even any family birthdays in August. She did send a few encouragement and thinking-of-you cards to those she heard were going through rough patches for one reason or another. For no particular reason, she sent one to Morgan. She subscribed to an encouragement pack of greeting cards from Fair Hope Notes and loved getting a new collection of cards in the mail each month. She always opened and looked through them immediately, then watched carefully for opportunities to pop one in the mail. She noticed it was almost time to get more stamps.

Lesson Two: Be Intentional

"Emotional Capacity is the next thing to write on your model," she instructed Morgan as they started their next session. She had included a sketch in the card she'd mailed him last week. They briefly reviewed the authenticity piece of the model and then began to explore the concept of emotional capacity. "After working to increase your awareness and coming into authenticity, it might actually seem that things are getting worse instead of better," she warned him. "Without awareness, we tend to spend so much of our lives avoiding what we don't want to feel, we seldom pay attention to what we do want to feel. But now that you are more aware and becoming more authentic, you'll find yourself moving up (on the ladder) and moving out bravely and authentically into situations with increased emotional capacity."

She then explained how she'd learned to flip her emotions over to find the equal, opposite, and desirable emotions in her awareness, as well.

He listened intently as usual, and then seized his chance to summarize.

- When climbing up and down the ladder of authenticity, the V widens and narrows, indicating my emotional capacity.
- When I am more authentic I move up, widening my capacity for all emotions.
- When I am less authentic I move down, narrowing my capacity for emotions.
- When I am high, with widened capacity, I may feel things are worse than before if I focus on the uncomfortable emotions versus the desirable ones.
- The direction I look (to the right or left) as I climb determines how I will feel. My dominant emotional state is determined by my focus.

She then asked him to come up with an example.

"When I focus on losing my mom," he began slowly, "being here alone, in this house, continuing to run her business, taking care of her horses and dogs, it can feel so empty." He paused and she waited. "I can pull away from it all, becoming less authentic, moving down on the ladder, and isolate myself from all the emotions. This will help me quit feeling that profound sadness."

Yes, that is one option, she observed to herself as he continued.

"If I remain high on the ladder, more authentic and fully aware, yet continue to focus on all that emptiness, I will eventually notice I feel a deep longing, some emotional pain, a lot of regrets, injustice, anger, bitterness, doubt, etc. My choice when I notice all that is to either isolate, as I already mentioned — or flip all those feelings over and look for their opposites. I can choose to remain authentic and shift my focus to the more desirable emotions like intense love, gratitude, faith, hope, relief, peace, appreciation, and even admiration and confidence."

They discussed how it is naturally so much easier to notice the negative emotions and then try to push them away due to the pain. But they also discussed the danger of pushing them away. When we isolate from the surface pain, we take steps down on the ladder of authenticity. When we take steps down on the ladder, we move away from our capacity for the desirable emotions as well.

"They always rise and fall in equal capacity, Morgan. Watch for it. It is always true."

She told him then about flipping the coin, finding equal value on both sides. The other side is always there in equal measure. They decided it might help Morgan as he was becoming familiar with the capacity concept to rate his negative emotions on a scale of 1-10. If he noticed a negative feeling of abandonment at an 8, he could then expect to find its opposite of at least an 8 as well.

Chapter 8

Going Deeper

Straight to the Heart

She knew the next concept she needed to share with Morgan, but still didn't know what to call it. It was a horizontal line across the model like a platform on which one moves around into both sides of emotional capacity — positioned at whichever level of authenticity one is operating. This platform concept was something deeper than she'd ever been able to name, and since she'd never taught the model before, it had never been fully labeled.

She thought about how it had been presented to her. She reviewed her journals, looking at her own path. Like everything else, she'd learned this over time by journaling, sketching, and gathering clues. She felt that if she simply continued to lay out the same path that had been laid for her, she could continue to guide Morgan.

By noticing her emotions, she'd come to recognize things that resonated with her. She decided to start there. Staying true to this one-foot-in-front-of-the-other strategy, she retrieved a well-worn copy of a poem from her bulletin board, *The Bridge Builder*, by Will Allen Dromgoole. There was something about it that had caused her to cry when she'd first read it several years before. She intended to read the poem to Morgan to start their next session, as an example of something that had resonated with her spirit early on in her transformation. Its message was an obvious inspiration for dubbing the little man her Bridge Builder, and now that message resonated more than ever. Not only did it perfectly describe his role in her life, now she was beginning to see herself as a bridge builder, too.

"Do you remember the little quote I asked you to pass along to your mom when I gave you the card at the conference?" she asked Morgan as they began.

"Go within or you'll go without," he replied.

"Do you remember if that resonated with you at the time?" she explored further.

He was silent.

She waited.

"What does it mean to resonate?" he asked eventually.

She laughed sweetly. *No problem. I'll back up a step.* "It just means that you deeply agree with it, in a way you can't really explain. We resonate with something in our heart, our gut, or our spirit, but not usually in our head."

He nodded. "No, I don't remember it resonating with me, but something about it must have resonated with Mom because I do remember her emotional state visibly changing when I told her."

This was encouraging feedback for her faith — a bonus. It had been difficult to deliver that message when it didn't make sense to her to do so. This next concept of the model moved into the realm of faith, and faith, she was discovering, usually came without any tangible feedback or logical explanations whatsoever.

"I'd like to read you a poem that *resonates* with me. I almost always get a tear in my eye or get a little choked up when I read it. I more fully understand that emotional reaction now, but the first time I read it, I had no idea what was going on."

The Bridge Builder

BY <u>WILL ALLEN DROMGOOLE</u>[1]

An old man going a lone highway,
Came, at the evening cold and gray,
To a chasm vast and deep and wide.
Through which was flowing a sullen tide
The old man crossed in the twilight dim,
The sullen stream had no fear for him;
But he turned when safe on the other side
And built a bridge to span the tide.

"Old man," said a fellow pilgrim near,
"You are wasting your strength with building here;
Your journey will end with the ending day,
You never again will pass this way;
You've crossed the chasm, deep and wide,
Why build this bridge at evening tide?"

The builder lifted his old gray head;
"Good friend, in the path I have come," he said,
"There followed after me today
A youth whose feet must pass this way.
This chasm that has been as naught to me
To that fair-haired youth may a pitfall be;
He, too, must cross in the twilight dim;
Good friend, I am building this bridge for him!"

---

[1] This is a real poem written approximated 1931 by Will Allen Dromgoole

They sat in silence for a few moments while she composed herself slightly, and then she continued. "Sometimes when I resonate with something, I sense a rush of gratitude, joy, or complete peace, but more often than not, I cry without explanation. When I sense an emotion like this, without any conscious understanding of the connection, I know that thing is *resonating* with my spirit."

He couldn't think of any examples, but he commented on the poem and how fitting it seemed. The chasm, he said, reminded him of the V in the model and the vast space to cross was the space of emotional capacity. "And you have crossed it ahead of me," he finished. "Thank you."

"You're welcome, Morgan, very welcome."

She went on to explain that she had come to know that this part of the model was deeply connected to things like this poem that resonated with her. She explained that Morgan didn't have to go looking for things that resonated, but he should just begin to notice them when they did, like clues to his spirit, his inner man. She suggested he keep track of them in his journal and let her know what he discovered.

"So, how is this concept different from authenticity?" he asked cautiously. "It sounds like another way of saying the same thing."

She knew this would come up. She'd asked herself the same thing many times. "The only way I can think of to explain it," she offered, "is that authenticity is what we can notice in our awareness, and this inner spirit concept is below the surface, almost completely hidden from our consciousness. When something connects with it, we can feel it, but we can't really wrap our head around it. It is deeper than our authenticity. It's like authenticity is the part that is above ground or conscious, and this is the part below ground: the roots, the unconscious."

"So, it's our core?" he suggested.

She nodded. Maybe that was the word she'd been searching for. She knew it would come and fit completely into place in time.

It always did.

They talked a bit longer about the definitions of spirit, and core, and resonate, then she decided to move on to the application.

She explained to him that as he began to move up in authenticity and his emotional capacity widened accordingly, he would notice the broader range of emotions could be difficult to maneuver through at times. She told him about times when she'd be experiencing a fantastic day, with lots of amazing experiences, and then get absolutely blindsided by a wave of unwanted emotion, seemingly out of nowhere. "But this," she explained half-apologetically, "is the price we pay for living authentically."

"But you are aware of it, so you know what to do?" he asked hopefully.

"I know what to do in my head," she answered, "but today we are talking about what we do in our heart in those moments, and how we make the heart and the head agree with each other. I've thought of many words for it, but none of them have completely fit my understanding of it just yet, so I continue to explore it."

The Core

They talked about how she'd come to see this level of faith as resilience, as a foundation, as an anchor, as a root system, as bedrock, as the center or core of our being. They discussed that it was the part of us we are unaware of, but that our Creator is fully aware of and wants to reveal to us, the way He sees us, but we don't see it yet.

They decided to wrap up there.

Morgan would continue journaling, noticing clues and exploring what resonated inside him for a couple weeks; they would re-open the topic later. After they prayed together and ended their session, she went to her own journal and thought about what was next. She thought of the times she'd acted out in faith, just knowing somehow she was to do something that defied logic. She'd delivered that Easter lily to the family across the street several years ago, way before she knew about any of these concepts. Something in her simply resonated with small, simple gestures with no strings attached; she truly had no expectations other than to surprise someone else with a little bit of joy or encouragement.

Just a few months ago, when she'd been shopping for the Father's Day cards, she'd had an interaction with Jim at the store that revealed a glimpse of her core. (Maybe she would settle on calling this her Core.)

Jim had spent quite a while in the same aisle with her that day, changing out another display, fairly close to her. He studied her as she read each Father's Day card thoroughly, choosing just the right two cards for her sons.

At one point, she stopped to acknowledge him. "How is your Saturday, Jim?" she greeted him by name.

"Oh, fine, thanks," he replied, picking up his box to move to another part of the store. "You absolutely amaze me," he commented. "Most people just run in here, grab a card, and run right back out the door. But you actually read them like you mean to say these things to someone in person. The people you send them to must really be special to you."

Looking back at that day showed that she was indeed acting from something deeper than a rationalized, authentic state. She recognized she was being fully present, fully alive, acting in full authenticity, with full emotional capacity, and in complete agreement with her spirit: her core identity. She noted all this in her journal and then wondered what else she still had to discover about herself.

Accountability

When they met again Morgan had a list of wonderful experiences to share with her, but she could sense after a few minutes of his enthusiastic monologue he was forcing himself to gain her approval that day.

As his report began to trail off, she decided to call him out on the things he seemed to be ignoring, reminding him to embrace them, not to avoid the whole picture even if it seemed painful.

He broke.

She'd called him out and didn't know if she'd done the right thing. She could tell he was sobbing. She prayed quietly and held space for him. He composed himself and chuckled a little bit at his vulnerability, admitting that indeed he had felt the need to pretend to be happy today. He didn't know why, he said, so she assured him that was not relevant. After the honesty and some gentle exploration of his emotions, she was able to share some scriptures, recommend a song for later, and then pray over him, ministering to his deep loneliness and comforting him in a way he would have never thought to ask for.

He felt refreshed and encouraged. They were able to start over, talking again about what had resonated with him over the past two weeks, noting the patterns that were emerging in his journaling.

"It always helps me to summarize it," he offered, and she could tell he was looking through his notes on the other end of the phone as he listed things off.

- Authenticity is my awareness of myself, I measure this on the little ladder as I move up and down, based on an awareness of my current state. This is me being my best, truest self.
- As I am more authentic, I move higher and then have access to a wider emotional capacity, the capacity for both desirable and undesirable emotions, pleasure and pain, joy and grief, in equal increasing or decreasing measure.
- Because God has the full range of these emotions, I do too, because I'm created in His image.

- I can feel any or all of those emotions based on my focus. I will always feel what I focus on, but I can assign or reassign the meaning however I choose to adjust my state.
- Now, to the core (if that's what we decide to call it) — the things that resonate — this is what allows me to fully embrace life at my current level, without getting my feet taken out from under me by the ebb and flow of the emotional tides.

What a joy it was to have such a motivated mentee! She knew when he summarized like this, from his own notes, that he was truly doing his work between sessions. She knew he was practicing and living in integrity because she was beginning to see his transformation.

The Bridge

There was another part of this she needed to draw out for him. "I actually like to picture it this way," she began. "Will you sketch a model on your page there before I start?"

He did.

"Now," she instructed, "go ahead and draw a dot or a little stick man about ¾ of the way up the ladder, and then draw a nice horizontal line across the emotional capacity, all the way from left to right, like a bridge. Do you see all the capacity for desirable emotions he has access to on the left and all the less desirable emotions he has off to his right? I like to draw a little smiley face on one side and a frown on the other, but that's up to you."

"Got it," he said.[2]

She continued, "What if that horizontal line is a strong, reinforced beam about 10 feet wide and strong enough to hold an elephant? He's going to be pretty confident moving back and forth with those emotions all day, no matter what comes at him, 'hell or high water,' so to speak. Right?"

---

[2] the journal sketch on YouTube: https://www.youtube.com/watch?reload=9&v=QHAGtxnBmis&feature=youtu.be

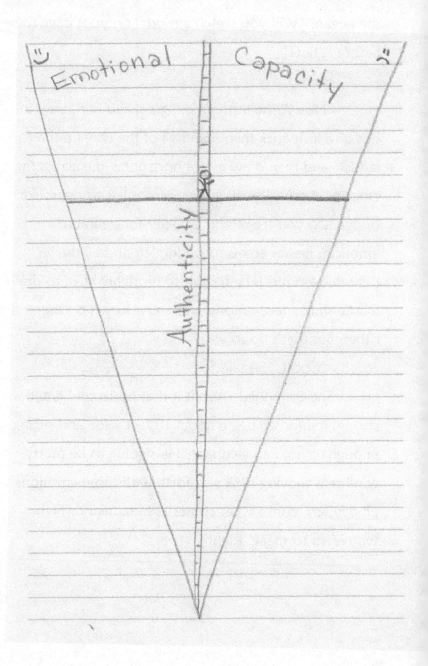

Morgan agreed, commenting that it's like the load capacity of a bridge. *Nice analogy,* she thought. *The horizontal line is a bridge.*

"But, what if," she continued, "that horizontal line is more like thin ice or a tightrope one must maneuver onto get out into those emotions instead? What good does one's authenticity and emotional capacity do them now if they must just hold tightly to the ladder, spending all their energy on awareness and focus, never feeling safe to move around and enjoy life at this level? If one can't trust the strength of the platform at this level, they will either stay a spectator, or they will retreat back down to a level that feels safe. We all will retreat back to whatever level resonates with us. That might be one rung, or six, but we will not stay for long at a level that doesn't resonate. When we retreats back to that former place of safety and strength, we can again enjoy our life at that level of emotional capacity and authenticity. It is not a bad thing, but there is more for anyone and now they have tasted it. If they can find a way to bring this core identity into agreement with that new level, anyone can try it again and might find that the bridge feels sound this time.

Perhaps as soon as the bridge feels strong, they are able to enjoy a full, rich life."

"This is resonating now!" Morgan said with a chuckle.

It was resonating with her, too. As she explained it, it described perfectly what she had felt at the conference when Morgan wanted her to mentor him. She had stepped up a rung, it didn't feel safe, she retreated to do her work, and now, here she was; even a step higher than where she was at the conference. She kept this story to herself for now, this session was to focus on Morgan, the notes she took for herself would help her expand on this idea later.

She decided to read an entry from her own journal to Morgan then, something she didn't do often, explaining it was written just before she'd become a published author.

I notice feelings of inferiority today, the entry began, *but I recognize that this is not in agreement with the way God sees me. I feel it, but it doesn't resonate. Like a shirt that is too tight, I don't like it. It doesn't fit.*

I must flip it over. What is in agreement with God in this? Inferiority is an emotion needing my attention, but it is no longer a part of my identity. I wish to release it and loose it from me. In its place I choose to identify with: Regal.

I am a child of God. I am the righteousness of God in Christ. I am a joint heir with Christ . . . I am Regal.

She stopped then.

He said he liked the analogy of it being like a shirt that didn't fit. "Can I just say something funny?" he asked. "We are always so serious when we get together."

"Of course! Please do." This wasn't the first time she'd been accused of being all business.

"I've been going through all the stuff in my mom's kitchen cupboards," he began, "and, oh my goodness! I'm trying to figure out why she kept all these little folded-up pieces of used aluminum foil — it's literally stuffed everywhere. I have to say, it really doesn't resonate with me and it's all getting thrown away!" Morgan laughed affectionately.

She laughed at his anecdote too, noticing the laughter resonated. She prayed with Morgan as they wrapped up their time. Next time, she was making the drive to his house. He had invited her several times, and their schedules had finally matched.

After she hung up, she poured another cup of coffee, got a sweater to brace against the September wind, and stepped out onto the back porch. She remembered the season of her life when she'd written about that inferiority in her journal. Her story had just been accepted for printing in the compilation book of stories and she was comparing herself to the other contributing authors. Some of them were already recognized speakers and authors. But as she wrote about it, inferiority began to sound like it did not belong to her, and she had been able to notice it, call it out, and disarm it. When she'd looked for the opposite emotion to fill its space, she found several: honorable, respectable, royal, etc. But she had most resonated with Regal. She didn't worry about why it resonated; resonation doesn't answer that question. She just tried it on and it fit, so she wore it every day now to remind inferiority it no longer had a place in her identity. She had outgrown it.

Chapter 9

The Space

Between the stimulus and the response is a space;
therein lies my freedom.

Surprise

She spoke to Morgan before she left her house to
drive to his; it was two weeks later. It had not rained so
her vehicle should be fine traversing his country road,
but her cell phone might not work if she got lost, so she
was being especially careful. He seemed very overjoyed
to hear from her. He mentioned he had a surprise.
Surprises definitely resonated with her, and she
anticipated it the entire drive.

When she arrived without incident, he was
thrilled to see her and took her immediately on a tour
of the barn and kennels before going into the house.
His mom had raised German Shepherds and had trained
some of them for service dogs. As he showed her
around, he explained he'd have to decide soon if he

would keep the place, or if he'd need to find another way to make his way in the world. "I thought it was all about money at first," he admitted, "but now I'm exploring it on a deeper level, thanks to you."

He gently pushed open the door to a large, separate room in the barn, and her heart leapt. It seemed like a dozen puppies were cuddled up next to their mother, wiggling and nursing.

"Oh, my!" she exclaimed softly. "How old are they?" She didn't know much about dogs.

"Only eight days," he said. "I'd like you to pick one."

That was a rung she'd not expected to climb today! "How sweet, Morgan. I'll have to give that some thought. I've never thought about having a dog."

"Never?" He seemed surprised. "You are the perfect candidate. You have the time, the space, and the heart for it."

She let herself open up to the idea. "I promise. I will definitely give it some thought."

Reframing

After seeing the whole place, enjoying a light
lunch of grilled cheese sandwiches and tomato soup,
they sat together in his living room. It was his idea this
time to get right down to business. He wanted her to
leave in plenty of time to get home before dark, and
she appreciated his thoughtfulness.

"Have you heard of reframing?" she asked him.
After deciding he didn't know the term as she intended
to use it, she continued. "It's been studied and reported
that the physiological components of being nervous are
almost identical to the feelings of being excited," she
explained. "So, if that is true, we have access to both of
those feelings when we feel the physical sensations of
butterflies in the stomach, dry mouth, or sweaty palms
before walking on stage to give a speech."

She confessed to Morgan this still happened to
her each and every time she got ready to speak at a
conference. She explained how she had trained herself
to reframe the meaning of the feelings. "It's quite
natural to feel anxious about something that hasn't
happened yet, especially if there are a lot of unknowns.
But if I take a moment to become aware of what I'm

feeling, I then have the power to choose a different meaning and a different feeling from within my current range of emotions. I can intentionally choose one that more fully resonates with my core identity. This little triad process is called reframing," she finished.

She reached out then and asked if she could draw something in his journal.

He handed it to her.

She wrote: ***focus > meaning > feeling***, and handed it back to him.

"A man named Lance Wallnau teaches this as the *triad of transformation*, and it fits perfectly right here," she concluded.

"So, you're headed to speak at a conference," he offered with understanding. "You are very high on the authenticity ladder and your emotional capacity is wide, so you are feeling a 10 out of 10 nervousness."

She'd almost forgotten he was using this rating scale to help with awareness, and was excited to see him use the technique so automatically.

He continued, "So you have the capacity for a 10/10 excitement, too, because of equal capacity. So the choice is yours and you'll be able to make that choice with grace and poise if it also resonates with your core identity."

"Exactly! My core identity agrees that I'm able, I'm powerful, and I'm anointed to do this work, so the choice is mine — IF I'm aware of the choice."

"So the little quote you sent me by text yesterday — that was for today's lesson?"

"Yes. It's my own paraphrase from some of the writings of Viktor Frankl."

Morgan turned back a page in his journal to see where he'd written it.

She joined him in saying it out loud. *"Between the stimulus and the response is a space; therein lies my freedom."* She raised her eyebrows and nodded to him, encouraging him to share his thoughts.

"The recognition of awareness and authenticity and capacity all leads up to this application, then. We do all this work in this little space between the stimulus and the response." He put his pencil down and put his hands up in the shape of a V. "The space of emotional capacity that widens and narrows as we move up or down – that is this space," he said.

"Yes, and most of the time we step right over it like a crack in the sidewalk, instead of seeing the power that could be ours. If we will simply increase our awareness of the space, we can choose and feel so much more empowered in our actions, our responses, and our emotional state. We will be acting in alignment with our core identity and that is a very empowering feeling. It is operating in self-control, one of the fruits of the Spirit, just like Jesus did."

"What is the other thing you texted? P - A – S?" he asked.

"I pronounce it Pause, and it simply stands for Personal Awareness of the Space," she explained. "It's what I came up with to help me remember to stop and notice the space when something didn't feel right or didn't seem to fit."

She referred back to reframing nervousness or anxiety, and explained how the external situation actually forced her up a rung on the authenticity ladder. "When we notice we've been forced up a level or two, our knee-jerk reaction is to identify fear, and then immediately back down to get away from it. But," she continued to encourage him, "a situation is never fully accessed by its initial emotions, in this case nervousness. Most of the time when we stop to identify our full range of emotions, there are a lot of positive and more desirable emotions equally available to us."

He put his hand up for her to stop a minute and then looked up when he was done writing. "So when I truly take a PAS, Personal Awareness of my Space, it helps me see the whole picture, find what resonates, and then act from my *intentionally chosen* emotional state. It's exactly what we talked about way back when we discussed awareness. What we own, can't own us."

She nodded and then emphasized, "But without awareness of the space there is no choice at all; without it we simply react. Stimulus. Response. Stimulus. Response."

"So, you're not just pretending to be brave. You truly are no longer afraid, because you've chosen a different meaning, and you are now feeling a completely different emotional state," he summarized.

Yes!

She then asked him to put his journal down and stand up. Once they were both standing, she began again, "I'm going to teach you something to practice when you are putting this all together, so please just follow along."

He jumped around a little like loosening up his muscles for an athletic event, and she laughed. He had some fun in his core, and she liked it.

She looked to the ceiling, raised her hands straight up above her head, and then opened them wide into a V. She instructed him to tip his chin up, close his eyes, and take several deep, cleansing breaths.

Afterward he laughed. "Wow, that really changes the old blood flow!"

"Yes, it changes everything. Anytime we change our physical posture, we'll notice our mental and emotional states shifting as well. It's like they become flexible or pliable, so it's a great thing to do when you begin and/or end your journaling time."

She then explained how she used the power pose to release the undesirable, ill-fitting things from her space, then to recognize and own the things she knew agreed with the Holy Spirit.

After discussing the applications for a minute or two, she looked at the clock to see if she had time for a little more, and decided she did. They sat back down and he picked up his journal again.

"Years ago, before I began my transformation," she shared, "I was very withdrawn and isolated. I know you read about that in the book. I was not in the right posture at that point in my life to give to others. I was totally closed up, physically, mentally, spiritually, and emotionally. There was no flow. If we want to make a difference in our own life, we have to look to how we can help others. We have to start the flow by getting all the yucky stuff out of the way if we want to open ourselves up to receive God's love and then be a vessel for Him to flow through. I don't think most people realize how closed up they are sometimes. I know I didn't realize it, but the power pose helps me remember to stay open, to release the junk, and to let the good stuff grow up and out of me."

"I like it," he said. "It gives me something to add to the journaling, something a little more tangible and active. I like it a lot!" He wrote one final thing and set down his journal. She waited so they could wrap up in prayer.

"Before you go," he said, "I've been wanting to tell you, I've been reading more about the fruit of the spirit and thinking about them as emotional states. They really do seem to resonate when I'm rating emotions and shifting states. I find I'm choosing them above most other words I used to choose. Like, I used to find myself wanting to feel happiness, friendship and companionship, or provision a lot, but not so much anymore. Those things are nice and I still identify them, but the things that really resonate if I'm being aware of everything in the space, are the fruits of the spirit. You mentioned self-control a minute ago and that is an amazing state to think about. So is love. Everything else just seems to fall into place underneath them. So, anyway, I'm just really getting a lot of mileage out of that list, and I wanted to share that with you."

"That's amazing, Morgan!" She reminded him of the last time they met and she'd called him out for not being honest about his emotional state.

He remembered.

She explained that this was a "space" she'd chosen to explore, pushing into him as she did that day. She said she just sensed something wasn't quite right, and she decided to pause in the space to notice it. Then, she'd acted from an intentionally chosen emotion: love.

He told her he was glad she had, and asked her if she'd please always call him out on things like that. Then he brought up the puppy again, wondering if she was ignoring a space of her own with her initial hesitancy.

"I'm not sure," she responded, laughing at his ability to turn the tables and coach her a little. "But I promise I'll explore it to see if it fits."

They talked about the time frame to take a new puppy home, and discussed what she'd need to have ready if she did decide to take the leap into responsible pet ownership. They prayed together and she got on the road. She would be home before dark and, yes, she'd text him when she got there safely. *Kids!*

Chapter 10

Deeper and Stronger

The same dream that dominates my waking hours
will be with me in the dark.
- Andy Andrews

Dreaming of Christmas

It was late October, the time of year she had always liked least because of Halloween; it just didn't resonate with her, she realized. Instead of fighting it now she simply released it easily and tuned into what she did love: Christmas! She and Morgan texted almost daily now, and her puppy was getting big. Yes, of course she was getting the puppy. She'd chosen a little male with a very calm disposition. Morgan said he appeared wise and contemplative and she told him it sounded more like an owl than a puppy.

She'd been in deep thought now for several weeks, considering the best name for him. She thought about Owl but it didn't fit. Maybe she'd just call him Surprise, she shared with Sandra one day as they chatted over coffee.

"He's purebred, isn't he?" Sandra asked. "You could call him Sir Prize!"

She liked it. It was cute, clever, simple, and she did resonate with surprises. She would try it on this weekend when she went to visit him again, to see if it fit.

All this was on her mind as she browsed at the card store that day for a few birthday cards. She focused on the fact that right beside the fall décor, Christmas was waiting to burst into its full angelic glory any moment. She'd loved Christmas her whole life and had no idea how she'd ended up marrying two men who hated it. Her first husband was the epitome of Ebenezer Scrooge, even as a pastor. Her second husband hadn't been as much so, but he certainly didn't share her exuberance. She wanted the entire season to start as early as possible, and then she wanted to milk it to the very last drop. Jim gave her space as she browsed, intently reading the birthday cards as usual. When she was ready to check out with the three cards, Jim greeted her with a hug that had become routine. Had she seen the new line of cards with the little owls? Jim wanted to know. Yes she had, as well as the ones with the silver Bible verses and the little hedgehogs too.

These were the simple pleasantries of a budding relationship and they volleyed naturally during the checkout transaction.

As she waved goodbye to Jim, she checked to see where she was meeting Sandra for dinner. They needed to talk about several things, and an evening meal worked better this time. The women she traveled with were planning a one-day Christmas Gala event to finalize their end-of-year mission funding goals. Sandra was helping with the event planning and organization. Sandra had already let her know they wanted her to be the keynote speaker, and she'd accepted, so dinner was mostly to talk about other things.

The first time Sandra had asked her to speak to the ladies' brunch, it had not gone particularly well. She recognized, looking back now, it was like being at a new level walking on a tightrope, maneuvering on a fragile platform. She hadn't known much about reframing or her core identity then, either, but the saving grace was that the brunch wasn't very well attended, so she'd not suffered too much humiliation and it had helped her realize other women did relate to her insecurities and authenticity quite well. From one of the women attending that day had come the invitation to write her testimony and submit it for the book, and the rest was now history.

She had written and polished up the story she'd shared at the brunch, and soon after it was chosen to be published together with other women's stories from area churches. One year later, she found herself traveling around the world with this group of ladies, speaking at various conferences and women's retreats. They told their stories, sold books, and raised funds for the missions' projects several of the women were supporting. She had gone along for the ride, so to speak, and found she was enjoying herself thoroughly. Next year, if they continued to travel that much, she'd have her dog to consider and make arrangements for, but the thought of it ignited little sparks of joy, so she knew it would all be okay. It fit.

Speaking of fit, she found herself mentally wandering more than usual today. She was at the table with Sandra, but realized she hadn't been fully present. She intentionally brought herself back to the agenda, but was again distracted with all the bustling around them and the thoughts in her head. "I'm so sorry. I feel so distracted today," she told Sandra, who then asked her to talk it out. Maybe that would help.

She tried that and ended up realizing she was completely uncertain of where to go next in her mentoring with Morgan. Sandra suggested that perhaps they were done. Roles change and seasons turn. If there was nothing else to tell him, and he had no pressing concerns or issues that needed addressing, perhaps it was just time to wrap up. This was a new thought and it would certainly get some of her journaling time that night. On the way home, she realized something else that was bothering her. Expectations. Regrets. Christmas always brought both, along with the opportunity to be too busy for them. They wouldn't hide from her this year. They would get some attention very soon.

This Christmas, she decided, nothing was going to limit her from being her best self — her most authentic, most spirited, most compassionate, most surprise-loving, encouraging, little-acts-of-service – self. She allowed herself to dream about these aspects of her core identity all the way home. Three years ago, she had started going to an all-night restaurant near the interstate on Christmas Eve, ordering soup and then leaving a $100 bill for her server. She loved just thinking about how much that money probably meant to the recipient. She didn't ever think about finding a way to see the reaction or get a thank you. She only did it for the surprise factor. This year she'd been saving a little money each month to do something else she'd always dreamed of. She was going to be a Secret Santa. She would go to one of the local department stores and anonymously pay off a couple of lay-a-ways that would otherwise not be picked up on Christmas Eve.

The Work

That night she sat alone with her journal and the few items she didn't want to ignore. She found herself pondering what was spiritual and what was emotional. She found herself staring off into space instead of writing, and as she did, hearing some words from another author, but they weren't coming from her mind. They were in her heart, resonating, trying to connect with something outside, softly, gently pushing their way into her consciousness. Her pencil slowly slipped from her fingers as she drifted off to sleep. The words kept coming,

I will lay my head on my pillow at night, happily exhausted, knowing that I have done everything in my power to move the mountains in my path. The same

dream that dominates my waking hours will be with me in the dark. Yes, I have a dream. It is a Great Dream and I will never apologize for it . . . Andy Andrews' voice continued speaking to her, around her, through her, from her core as she slept.

When she awoke an hour later, she remembered the words and wondered how long it had been since she'd re-read the book *The Traveler's Gift* or listened to the audio version of *The 7 Decisions*. She needed to recommend them to Morgan, she decided. They had impacted her deeply and she wanted something valuable to give Morgan this weekend. She texted Morgan about it right away so she wouldn't forget it, knowing he'd already be asleep and would find the message in the morning. She set down her phone and turned off the bedside lamp. As she did, she glanced at Sir Prize's bed in its new place ready for him, right near her nightstand.

The next morning, she was very aware of her space. She had become an avid reader (and audio-book listener) since cracking open that first Brene Brown book, so it was not unusual for her to hear her favorite authors' voices mixed into her morning affirmations and self-talk. Much like the words she'd heard the night before, they often sounded like they came from her heart rather than her mind.

As she prepared for the day, she noted all the affirming and energizing quotes buzzing around in her mind and in her heart. They were like the sounds coming from a fireplace, crackling and spirited. She heard Brene Brown encouraging her to "Lean in." Andy Andrews was nudging her to "Be a person of action." She felt prodded to "Press in for the upgrade," as Graham Cooke would say, and she heard "Embrace it all," from the Bridge Builder.

Bible verses mixed in with the quotes that morning and she felt a new delight in the richness of the mixture. It was igniting her sensitivity to the majesty and sovereignty of God. She had a sense her energy was delightful to Him. With this thought, she turned on a playlist of some of her favorite worship songs and actually danced for a bit, like no one was watching but Him.

Her morning journaling routine always started with awareness: *What do I see, hear, feel, know, and believe about God, myself, and the present situation?* After she'd written these things down, noting which ones resonated with her and agreed with the Holy

Spirit, she would usually stand in her power pose, lifting her hands. She prayed to release some of the unwanted things, for them to leave her, and then prayed to bind herself to the things God wanted to release through her.

Expectations and Regrets

Before entering the house, she and Morgan visited the barn, played with the puppies, and discussed her pup's new official given name: Sir Prize. It fit. Maybe she'd just call him Sir unless he was in trouble and needed both names. As they made their way from the barn to the house, Morgan told her he was glad she'd decided to take the puppy because this would be the last litter. It would not be a quick move, but he'd decided he wanted a more social life. He'd start looking for ways to move closer to the city. He said he was ready to let it all go now, not because of emotional baggage or regrets, but because he didn't think this was the life that fit him. She looked around at the beautiful ranch home, and wondered if it might fit her better than the city, but she quickly decided it would not.

When they finally sat to talk, the conversation naturally came back to his mother and the grieving process. "Grief has a way of shaming us about what we could have done differently, when it is far too late to make it right," she reflected. "Do you have many regrets?"

"Oh, yes, more than a few," he answered immediately and then looked at his journal, signaling her to wait while he wrote some things. "I regret not knowing my father. I regret the hatred my mother lived in, that she didn't find peace sooner. I regret a lot of things regarding the two of them. But I also regret not expecting more from myself because of my mom's bitterness. I bought into all this," he waved his arm across the large, sparsely furnished living area, "and it doesn't even fit me. I'm almost 30, and I've just realized it. That's difficult to swallow."

She felt sad listening to him, but she remained in peace, letting him talk through his full realization and verbally explore the space as it resonated with him. While he talked, she jotted several notes down, and so did he.

There was something she'd realized in her own journaling time this week, and even though it was still taking shape, this seemed a good time to share it. "I'm not at all sure how to best communicate this," she began. The whole concept of Resonating with the Core Identity was so deep and internal, it seemed that it almost couldn't be put into words, but she hoped the Holy Spirit would help with the interpretation.

"I'm observing that resonation, like other things on the emotional capacity model, works both ways. Sometimes things resonate because they are attracted to us, and sometimes they resonate to be released."

"This is even taking me to a new level," she shared. "I don't know much about bridges, but we keep referring to how strong or wobbly the bridge is when we attempt to move around at a new level. I wonder if when designing a physical bridge, they go deeper to make it stronger." Neither of them stopped to search it online, but they both liked the sound of it. They both took a few more notes and found some Bible verses that fit the notes.

He stood then and invited her to join him, "Shall we lock all this in?" She followed his lead. They both raised their hands and she listened as he prayed, releasing and establishing himself in alignment with the heart of God.

"Father God, I pray now and release all the regrets I've just spoken. I acknowledge, call out, and dis-identify with pride, regret, shame, excuses, blame, criticism, and all hopelessness." He listed several other things he'd written before continuing. "I now recognize the things from Your Spirit within me that more fully align with Your heavenly design for my life. I bind myself to Your love, Your admiration, Your delight in me, Your anointing and empowering work in me. I choose to be a vessel to overflow with Your fruit, Your love, Your joy . . . " When he finished, he stood with his eyes closed a few moments longer before coming back to her company.

Amen. Well done, she affirmed silently. She knew he didn't need to hear it from her. She knew God was smiling. She had a sense that Morgan had the favor of Heaven right now and it reminded her of Mary in the Christmas story. Mary had no idea what it meant to have the favor of God in her life, or where that road would take her; she was just authentic, open, and willing. Hope and expectancy filled the stillness.

Chapter 11

Hidden Value

*Genuine love must be the closest thing
to Heaven on Earth*

Value in the Regrets

The next time they spoke was the day she would take Sir Prize home with her. He got to come inside and cuddle up on her lap that day while she and Morgan talked. They didn't even talk about the fact that their roles were changing. They both just knew it had happened along the way. He began their conversation by asking her about the upcoming Christmas Gala event. He was curious if she was nervous at all.

It was only a few weeks away now, and she admitted she was nervous, but in a different way than she'd ever been.

He invited her to talk it out.

She explained that most of the ladies attending would be married, and would be attending with their spouses. She had been wondering how to present to them, saying she didn't think of herself as an expert in relationships, especially in marriage. "I don't feel it's important to talk about our past regrets very often, as you know."

"But, sometimes there is value in it — for the present," he reminded her.

True. She'd probably said that to him.

"So, tell me your story," he encouraged her, "the parts that weren't in the book. What's tripping you up? Maybe I can help you find the value."

Could she explore this with him? Maybe there was some value for her upcoming audience. Maybe there was also value for Morgan. She knew he wanted to find a wife someday, someone to love and cherish. She decided to climbed up a rung on the ladder, open herself to the increased emotional capacity, and explore bravely the bridge at that level. When she did, she found it was strong and safe.

She shared with him how she'd lived in utter isolation and numbness, merely going through the motions for several years after her husband passed away. She then shared with him about her initial hesitancy when he'd asked her to coach him. "That ministry part of your request spotlighted an unopened box in my past," she explained.

She continued, sharing the highlights of those painful years as a young pastor's wife. She shared about the dream where she'd emptied the old box. She expanded, telling him she'd actually had a nervous breakdown at that point in her life, and now she recognized it was the grace of God, providing her escape. She'd attempted suicide and had been sent to a "hospital." This was long before mental health counseling was acceptable for people in ministry positions as prominent as hers.

During her hospital stay, her husband had been caught drinking. He'd been hiding alcohol in his church office for a long time. He was immediately asked to seek treatment or leave the ministry, too. He'd reacted in a rage. He had walked away from the church, taken a railroad job, filed for divorce and won custody of the children. But soon, because he was gone too many hours and babysitting was difficult for him, her sons came to live with her in the tiny apartment she could barely afford working as a waitress in the city. She wasn't a single mom long before she began dating an office supply salesman who'd flirted with her at the restaurant, and then gotten her a corporate job in a high-rise building downtown. She'd married way too soon, she summarized, but for the most part it had worked out well. It had been a safe place for her to start over and it had provided a stepfather for her boys who would never fully understand their own father's disastrous course. Less than a year later, her first husband had been found dead from a heart attack; he was drunk. Their oldest son was only in kindergarten at the time.

She paused at this portion in the self-disclosure. They compared their lists of valuable aspects of her testimony, she acknowledged she was sensing some deep feelings of inadequacy. Maybe it was deep in her heart trying to get out. They decided she should work on it, right there in the space. She wrote some things down and so did he.

"Your authenticity is high, and your capacity is wide," he offered after she'd stopped writing, "so you are just determining your focus, reassigning meaning, and paying attention to what resonates."

She agreed, and then continued, "And then, I look to see what is in agreement with the Holy Spirit, in alignment with my core identity." She knew God was doing something deep in her right then. *Is this something new I want to be part of my identity, or something old, trying to get out because it no longer fits?* she asked herself. She wrote a little more, while he waited: *Joy, Freedom, Celebration, Connection, Friendship,* (and some new things) *Purpose, Adventure, Expectancy, Dreams!*

Then they stood together and raised their hands high.

When she finished praying, she was full of expectancy and enthusiasm. She felt almost pregnant with a gift, a surprise from God. Morgan stepped toward her, hugged her and kissed her cheek tenderly. She sensed his authenticity and imagined he would have shown this same tenderness to his mother. *Genuine love must be the closest thing to Heaven on Earth,* she decided. This feeling is what she had noticed during her morning quiet times recently, and it was the same almost-tangible closeness she felt in her encounters with the Bridge Builder. Maybe someday she'd tell Morgan about the Bridge Builder, but not today. Right now, she allowed the love to fill her, displacing all conscious and unconscious inadequacy.

When she turned to pick up her journal, Sir Prize was chewing on her pencil. The new level called Puppy Ownership had officially begun!

Morgan gave her a few more puppy instructions, loaded a bag of food into her vehicle, and waved as she started home. She would let him know when they arrived safely at home.

As she drove along, she mulled over the points of value they had come up with together. Prize slept beside her; maybe she'd call just him Prize except when he was in trouble. She was glad Morgan had thought ahead for her and acclimated the puppy to riding in a vehicle. Thinking ahead and being especially thoughtful were two of his particularly good qualities, she observed, and she wondered about a way to introduce him to her niece. No, being a matchmaker didn't resonate at all, so she let it go.

Obstacles

Nothing is as simple as it appears, she observed the next morning. She couldn't reach right for her journal now. The puppy had to go outside first. She didn't mind; she'd get back to it. When she did have him settled back in and picked up her chewed pencil, she had to laugh. He was cocking his little head and watching her; he did look just like an owl. She decided that name did fit him after all! She'd call him Sir Owl if he was in trouble, or just Sir!

She texted Morgan who immediately responded that he wasn't sir-prized at the change.

LOL! She shot back.

The day would be devoted to Owl, and when she could get back to it, preparation for her presentation at the gala. She'd decided to put together a workbook for everyone, about ten pages, and this way they could follow along while she introduced the model and told a few of her experiences exploring it. Morgan had given her permission to tell about their meeting and use that story if she thought it worked in. She thought through several others and then realized she was truly preparing more with her head than her heart. She sat and spent some time just focusing on her friendship with the Lord and the joy of her salvation. Majesty and Holiness were concepts that transcended her mind, so she'd found ways to use certain kinds of music that resonated deeply, and an ever-growing list of scriptures on her bulletin board to move intentionally from her head to her heart. She stayed there quietly until she was fully amazed and overflowing with gratitude for this full access to the presence of God.

Creative Process

From this place of worship and rest, she pulled out her computer and decided to prepare her speech as if she was giving specific instruction to Morgan. This way, she would keep it personal yet be fully authentic for everyone.

She'd talk to him about two tools for transformation: the model and the journal. She would touch on the whats and the hows and encourage him to risk leaving his comfort level and keep rising. And then she would do her best, with the Holy Spirit's help, to communicate the piece about the bridge and the core identity. She would also want him to know that a transformation is a life-long process rather than a one-time goal. The model and the journal are only tools, she would explain, but they are only as valuable as he would make them. He would have to put in the work to practice and hone the skills. His spiritual growth would always be directly tied to his emotional state; the two are inseparable, she'd remind him.

That was enough, she felt. It didn't have a conclusion yet, but she trusted that would come. She began to prepare the worksheet notes. She then thought about what she would wear and what arrangements she'd make for Owl, Sir Owl. She watched him sleep, his cute little black belly rising and falling. She hoped his owl-ness was only in mannerism and temperament. If he ended up nocturnal, sleeping all day and playing all night, she'd be finding another name.

Chapter 12

The Christmas Gala

When God made His way to us, He also made
our way to Him.

Butterflies were doing their routine somersaults
all over in her stomach as she took a breath. This was a
very special night.

"PAS," she told herself. She saw herself in grace,
in love, in service, in royal splendor reflecting well her
heavenly identity, and then she walked to the podium.

It was nearly Christmas. The conference room
was decorated in silver and gold with red and green
scattered throughout; the smell of pine and cinnamon
were subtle yet undeniable. Candles added to the
mystery. The musicians that had preceded her on the
stage had done a wonderful job of ushering the entire
audience into a peaceful, hopeful emotional state she
hoped would help catapult them into a mindset of
transformation.

Christmas is a season of heightened authenticity for many people. She observed that some even felt a sort of seasonal emotional capacity but without the self-concept to continue the generosity and cheer for long, they often slipped into a deep slump after the New Year. Her musings melted soon into a deep love for her audience. She connected with several faces with direct eye contact. Some were obviously tired and distracted, but others nearly screamed to her with hidden pain. She paused on those for a moment. Others shouted of hope and anticipation, empty journals and pens poised, wanting to hear everything she had to say.

She would tell her story a bit differently this time. Not because the story was any different, but because she was different. She knew her story last year on tour, but this year she knew herself in a deeper way, and that was the crux of the message now.

Each of these women had left their own families for a weekend during this Christmas season. They had chosen to be involved in a mission project they cared deeply about and had not only raised their own funds for that mission funding goal, but they had then raised their own personal funds to be here for this conference, all with the hope of taking home new insights to help them with real issues in their home churches.

She remembered a few time she'd attended conferences with other young pastor's wives and sat blankly, overwhelmed with the amount of pressure that came with the role and worried the whole time about her babies back home. She longed to see these women understand and love themselves in a new way, for their authenticity to bud and begin to grow. She wanted them to see who they really were, even if it wasn't pretty or comfortable at first. She knew some of them were walking wounded, hiding under pretend smiles and exhausted from the act. She knew this because she'd been there.

Many of them were pastors' wives and they had their best clothes on, their best emotions on their sleeves, and the rest of their pain tucked neatly away in boxes marked with big black letters, like hers had been.

Maybe their boxes read

SEMINARY *or*
THE FIRST FUNERAL DINNER: TOTAL FAIL *or*
THE SEVENTH MOVE

They were all here as women in ministry, many of them bringing their spouses with them for this part of the evening. She pulled back to span the entire crowd now, having realized all these thoughts in a few heartbeats, and she was overcome with emotion. The deep desire to give something of value to these eager hearts resonated from her. She was moved to tears before she could utter a single word.

As if on cue, an elderly gentleman from the front row stepped forward the few short steps to hand her a neatly folded handkerchief. She blinked the tears away and could hardly believe her eyes. Right there in front of her was the Bridge Builder! How in the world could she continue now?! She thanked him softly; the audience waited while she collected herself and stayed in love.

PAS, she thought, *PAS*.

"Pastors' wives, women in ministry, and other *Dear Ones*," she began, smiling warmly at him. She noticed her growing confidence. "I know you thought you came to hear my story tonight, but I think most of you already know it, so I want to take this chance to talk to you about your stories instead."

Her mentor sat throughout the entire session, writing notes in the workbook pages she'd provided for everyone, just like all the other members of the audience. She drew strength from him being there the same way she did when he wasn't visible, from within her.

Everything you need is within you now, she heard herself saying during the times of PAS. As she presented, she felt like she wasn't speaking, but that God was simply using her mouth. It fit. There was a bridge al each new level, she heard herself saying. A bridge that would hold them strong and secure at each level if they allowed the Holy Spirit to do His work: loosing and releasing the old and the new.

There had been a lot of meeting and greeting and networking at this special one-day Christmas event, but these women didn't need to leave here knowing other women better; they needed to know themselves better, and to do that, they would need a heart encounter with God.

She thought back about her own transformation and how she'd found that to be true. After she'd come to know herself a bit, she'd reached out to Sandra and formed a deep friendship there. Some of these women didn't yet have the capacity for that type of authentic friendship, but she knew they could and she knew how much it had enriched her own life.

She tried to look at each of the women in the room as she spoke, but most of them were writing. Those who weren't often had a tear in their eye, but not a tear of pain, she noticed. It was a tear of hope.

Because she was speaking authentically, because her capacity was so broad, and because everything she was speaking was resonating with her heavenly identity tonight, she felt almost out-of-body, like she was simply a messenger delivering a heavenly gift: a gift of pure love. That was the gift she'd received from the Bridge Builder: a bridge to pure love delivered directly from Heaven's heart.

"I want to challenge you as you continue to celebrate this Christmas season," she began to wrap up. "God handed us his dear Son, who willingly gave up Heaven in order to join us in our earthly experience. Now, He is asking each of us to give up this earthly experience, as we've know it, to join Him in experiencing Heaven on earth. Christmas brought us a gift from Heaven's heart, and then Easter came along and opened that bridge for full two-way access. Our

God doesn't do things halfway! When he made His way to us, He also made our way to Him!

"You know, it's funny how He's done so much for us, yet we still have trouble trusting Him at times. He asks us for our pain, and offers us something better. That's a good deal. He asks for our sorrow, and offers us joy in return. Another good deal! He asks us to give up our fears . . . and we think, Now, that's going too far!"

The audience laughed a little at this break in her monologue.

"At Christmas time, God allowed angels to be the messengers to tell others of His special gift. But you know, He never wanted the messenger to be more important than the message. I truly believe the message I've given you tonight is a gift directly from God to you. I am only the messenger. Our life is a gift from God and it is designed to be lived at full capacity."

She asked each of them to stand and then asked the musicians to return to the stage for their closing performance of the night. "Let's not wait for Heaven to live in a heavenly emotional state," she said in parting. "Let's enjoy Heaven on earth, at Christmastime and all through the year! Bless you all!"

The Bridge Builder was standing near the others in the front row when she exited the stage.

She still held his handkerchief in her hand. She carefully descended the four small steps backstage and paused to listen to the musicians. Then, there he was at the bottom of the stairs, waiting for her. His hand brushed hers as she handed him the handkerchief.

She thought about asking him if she could keep it, but she didn't. She wondered if this was all just a figment of her imagination, but she already knew better than that. *What similar doubts Mary must have entertained after her encounter with Gabriel*, she thought.

Saying nothing, they walked together, he a little behind her, through the hallway and then through the side door of the conference room near the book tables. They stood together beside an enormous Christmas tree as the musicians led the audience in a final worship set. She wondered how long he would stay.

She'd decided awhile back that she'd just come right out and ask him who he was if she ever saw him again, and as soon it was quiet enough, she intended to do just that. But when the song ended, the room was hushed with an extraordinary reverence. It sent chills up her arms. When she glanced at him, she knew he was leaving.

"Wait," she whispered, reaching out but not quite touching him. She placed both of her hands on her heart. "My name is Shirley."

She said it as if he didn't know who she was. After all these years of coming in and out of her life, in and out of her dreams, her home, her journal, in and out of her head, her heart, and her spirit . . . surely, he knew who she was.

Maybe she was saying it more for herself, because she finally knew.

When he smiled back at her, she felt complete love, as if he was smiling from inside of her. It was the same internal sense of love she had begun to feel a lot lately; every time she looked at someone with love, it felt just like this. This was Heaven!

She became aware that the audience was being dismissed and would soon be milling around them. She felt brave enough to now ask him. "Are you . . . " she began, but then it didn't really seem to matter anymore, so she didn't finish.

Characteristically, with a little touch of his elbows, he vanished. And, while she still basked in the heavenly love, she heard His gentle whisper in her spirit, "I AM."

Epilogue

Epilogue

The Bridge Builder beckons....

At the beginning of this book, I promised you something amazing. I promised you a bridge. Those are very important promises to me. They are so important in fact, I'd love to hear from you immediately. Will you text me, call me, or send an email right now? My personal cell phone is 308-629-7007, and my email is

ExpectingSomethingAmazing@gmail.com

I cannot wait to hear your story! I want to be sure you have whatever you need to put legs on the insights you've just gained. Some of you have already taken copious notes at the end of each chapter. Some of you are planning to re-read and take notes the second time. Some of you related more to the mentor, and others to the mentee. No matter, I want to hear from you.

The lessons Shirley received from the Bridge Builder and introduced to Morgan are simple, insightful and practical, but that does not mean they are easy to implement into your daily life. There's something inherently ironic about saying, "There's no wrong way to journal." The obvious opposite says, "There's no right way either."

So, how do you start? What do you do next?

Dust off an old journal and just start by noticing the moment:

What do I see, hear, feel, know, and believe about God, myself, or my situation right now?

Notice it; name it.

Download the Power Thesaurus app to help with the list.

Then, flip all these things to find their opposites: What would I rather see, hear, feel...

You're becoming more authentic and exploring wider emotional capacity, even now!

One of the most recurring themes in my work with clients around the world is the ongoing process of a life transformation. I can guarantee exploring the model with your own journal will yield transformational benefits in relationships, finances, spiritual intimacy, and overall life happiness. I also guarantee - the process will be an amazing one.

I'd love to show up in your living room while you're watching movies tonight, or write an encouraging note in your journal while you sleep, but I'm only human.

Don't wait for something dramatic or miraculous to start your journey. You can cross the bridge to your most authentic life, starting right now. Hope is beckoning.

Preview of the sequel

Authenticity Beckons: The Bridge Builder
Returns

10 years later –

His weathered hand reached down and rustled the dog's ears. His voice was gentle and encouraging, "It's ok, Owl. She'll pull out of this. It will be just fine. You'll see!"

He knew he was talking out loud to a dog, but this dog was used to being talked to. Morgan knew he was not really talking to the dog anyway, but was simply reassuring himself.

The two watched as the ambulance pulled deliberately away from the house and then picked up speed. "She's in capable hands," he said matter-of-factly. "She'll be just fine."

Sir Owl whimpered a little, and then followed back inside the house.

Morgan began to gather a few things she might need at the hospital, and then stopped short. In the corner of the room stood a frail little man, looking at Morgan with the warmest and most peaceful eyes he had ever seen...

Dear woman in ministry,

I didn't write this book; I received it. First, it was received as a love letter from the Holy Spirit to my spirit, and then it was published as a love letter to you, through my fingers. There were many times during the writing process I felt like I was reading the words instead of writing them. I couldn't wait to sit down, close my eyes, and type. I often had no ideas before I typed them. This experience has moved me in ways I cannot even communicate, and I pray it has done the same for you.

When I close my eyes and think of you, a woman in ministry, I see a Spirit-Filled Woman of God, full of favor, strong in faith, approved for good works, and attractive with the beautiful Fruit of the Spirit.

I do not know how you see yourself, but I hope through these pages, you've come to see yourself more clearly as all of Heaven sees you.

See your emptiness and your strength.

. . . your brokenness and your wholeness.

. . . your isolation and your authentic connections.

. . . your beginning and your end.

. . . your old identity, dead and buried, and your new identity, reborn and thriving.

You, dear woman of God, are blessed and highly favored; come and find rest for your soul.

I hope you are energized, encouraged, and refreshed from these pages and may your life never be the same. Please reach out and let me know how this work has touched you as well as what other needs you still have. I would love to connect with you personally, as an intercessor, a resource, a counselor, a speaker, or a sister in Christ.

In Authentic Love,

Beth

About the Author

Beth Trennepohl is a licensed professional counselor, author, and speaker. She is passionate about helping individuals live empowered and more satisfying lives. Drawing from her experience as a counselor, assisting with hundreds of life-transformations including her own, Beth's message is rich with pivotal and practical insights. She currently resides with her husband in Nebraska; the couple has raised two sons, and now they enjoy grandchildren as well.

Contact Information

Email: expectingsomethingamazing@gmail.com

Call or text: 308-629-7007

You can also find Beth on Facebook

(facebook.com/dearbeth)

Scheduling

Beth still sees clients in private practice, locally and online. She also hosts online topical groups to teach journaling mastery and other elements of her original Emotional Capacity Model. To find out more about these services, simply contact her.

As her schedule allows, Beth also loves to travel and would be honored to speak at your upcoming retreat, convention, or (her favorite) B&B retreats. Simply send her your uniquely crafted invitation via one of the methods above to begin to coordinate your schedule with hers. No matter the venue, she will inspire your group toward a practical life-transformation. Beth's ministry is not limited to Christian women, but these invitations are prioritized.

Special Thanks
and Shout-outs

A very special thanks . . .

To my husband for seeing me through my transformation, treating me like I was sane, and even acting interested as I discovered invisible bridges and spoke of intangibles like authenticity and capacity and identity over our morning coffee. Thank you for the swing time each day.

To my sons and their beautiful families: be inspired to do great things! If anyone can be great, we can all be great. Fear gets us nowhere. We were ALL born to be amazing.

To all my dear friends in public ministry and coaching: you have inspired me, healed me, and broken my heart with our shared angst: may you find the joy of authenticity, learn to embrace it all, and always go within.

To <u>Bryan Caison</u>, for not giving up. It's not over until you win.

To Brian Hardin and the Daily Audio Bible family. I love you every one!

To Og Mandino and Andy Andrews for teaching me my most profound and life transformational lessons in stories.

To Brene Brown and Lance Wallnau for always being the brave voices in my head.

To Graham Cooke for encouraging me through Game Changers and brilliant perspectives. You often say the same things I've just written, as if we have the same source. Oh, and in case no one had told you, you sound just like God!

To my dear friend Holy Spirit's original idea of 2018's Lent-Without-Limits; it changed me forever!

To the lifelong creative work of my Heavenly Father who built that first Christmas bridge to get Jesus to me, so I could in turn have full access to God. My intimacy with the triune God is both my purpose for being and the legacy I leave behind.

Additional Author Recommendations

Daily Audio Bible App

https://dailyaudiobible.com/

FairHope Notes

https://notesclub.com/join-the-club/

Jacquie Lawson Online Cards

https://www.jacquielawson.com/

Power Thesaurus App

Search your app store to download

Made in the USA
Monee, IL
25 June 2021

72061057R10104